CHOSEN BY A DRAGON

Fallen Immortals 4

ALISA WOODS

ISBN-13: 9798869392749

<h1 style="text-align:center">Chapter One</h1>

Two down, and an infinite sea of women to go.

Leonidas stood with his arms crossed, staring resolutely at the door of the small receiving room they had conjured just for The Mating Game he was playing. Only the stakes were far higher than any of the women waiting outside could possibly know.

"How am I going to do this?" he asked his brother with a sigh.

Lucian glowered at him. "You've only interviewed two women. It's way too fucking early to give up." His brother was the crown prince of the House of Smoke—correction, the *king* of the House of Smoke, now that a bastard of a dragon named Tytus had killed their father. Lucian had already found his mate, and Arabella's True Love and the dragonling it produced was supposed to be *enough*. Leonidas's freakishly adorable week-old nephew Larik was supposed to fulfill the ten-thousand-year-old treaty that kept the peace between the mortal and immortal realms. But apparently *no*... it had been revealed that all three dragon princes of the House of Smoke Lucian,

Leonidas, and their hopelessly lost-in-love brother, Leksander—had to find mates and successfully spawn dragonlings. And it wasn't just the lineage of the House of Smoke at stake. If the treaty fell, humankind would be at the mercy of immortals even worse than Tytus—including the fae, who were capricious and definitely *not* human-loving.

Leonidas squinted at his brother. "How did you do it? How did you make Arabella fall in love with you?" Because that was the key—Leonidas needed to win the True Love of a human woman, and not fall in love along the way, thanks to an angry witch and an ancient curse. He'd spent centuries perfecting his *Not Falling in Love* game, given he preferred to keep on living. The key to that was a constant stream of lovelies through his bed, hardly a horrific fate, although after a time truly numbing to the soul. No doubt that was the purpose of the curse. And after five hundred years, seduction was something he did automatically. But he'd never had to seduce a woman into fulfilling the treaty—that was Lucian's job. Leonidas's was simply to perform his royal duties and not lose his heart, no matter how beautiful or willing or sweet the woman. Get them into bed? Sure. Promise the world, knowing it would only last a night? Standard Operating Procedure. But convince them he was worthy of their True Love? Seduce them into a dangerous pregnancy? How the fuck was he supposed to do that?

And failure meant *death*. His and countless others.

"*Make* her fall in love?" Lucian asked, screwing up his face, like he thought Leonidas had already turned *wyvern*, the wild dragon form he would soon take, now that he was near the end of his natural lifespan. And ever since he'd been poisoned by Tytus, Leonidas's wyvern lurked even closer to the surface, a malevolent force just biding its time at the edges of his mind.

Lucian wasn't wrong to worry.

"I did everything I could to *stop* Arabella from loving me," his brother continued. "I was madly in love with *her*—you know that. But I was deathly afraid of—" Lucian looked away, but he needn't explain. Leonidas knew it well enough—his brother feared losing the woman he loved to the dragonfire sealing and then the carrying of his child, the very thing demanded by the treaty but that nearly cost Arabella her life.

It had been torment to watch the two of them go through it. The only saving grace in all the madness was that Leonidas would never have to suffer that himself. Even now. Sure, he needed to win a mate. And her love for him had to be True or none of it would work—the baby, the treaty, all of it. But absolutely, positively, under no circumstances could he fall in love with whatever hapless female he convinced to carry his child. If he did, that wyvern form—that wild-eyed, mindless dragon—would take over, and he would never see his own dragonling being born.

For much of the last week, he'd thought that might be preferable. Or more realistically… *unavoidable.* Leonidas had already resigned himself to that fate—only without the overwhelming pressure to leave a dragonling behind before he passed.

"Oh, I see," Leonidas said to his brother with a smirk. "Arabella simply fell in love with you with absolutely no effort on your part whatsoever. It must have been your irresistible charm and your spectacular form. Or are you just *that good* in bed, my brother?"

Lucian glared, and it was the first time Leonidas almost laughed in this whole bleak affair.

Instead, he just shook his head and dropped his gaze to

his black, polished shoes. "You know I would give anything to have what you have with Arabella," he said softly. Then he felt the full burden of this nightmare business settle on his shoulders like a boulder.

When he peered up, all the anger had fled from his brother's face. *"Leonidas."*

Leonidas held up his hand and forced the smirk back onto his face. "I've been cursed for a long time, Lucian. No need for pity now." He drew in a breath and pulled his gaze back to the closed door beyond which two dozen women waited for him to pick the not-so-lucky one among them to seduce into this wretched business of fulfilling the treaty. "But I do need your help, my brother. I am adrift in this without a lifesaver. In other words, I have no fucking clue what I'm doing." He turned back to Lucian.

His brother seemed to struggle for words, too many emotions rippling across his face to identify each fleeting one. His expression finally settled into a kind-hearted openness—and it twisted Leonidas's heart in recognition. Lucian had always been the deepest feeling of the three of them. The one with the softest heart, and the one most wounded by the burden that fell on him as crown prince. That he and Arabella had survived and made their love work renewed Leonidas's faith that anything was possible.

Lucian's hand landed on his shoulder, and somehow it lightened Leonidas's own burden. He could count on his brothers for anything—if they could help, they would. Especially Lucian.

"If love is meant to be, it will be," Lucian said. "If my time with Arabella, and even Cara before that, has taught me anything, it's that love is a force in the universe that has its own power. You'll find the one for you, Leonidas… and you'll no more be able to stop her than I could stop Arabella from the course she was determined to take."

"Only if I find a woman as stubborn as your mate," Leonidas said with a grin.

Lucian smiled. "You have centuries of practice, my brother. How many of the women who've passed through your lair have fallen in love with you? How many have you had to escort off the keep to ensure they actually left?" He smirked. "It's a matter of numbers before it happens again. Keep looking."

Leonidas sighed. "You're probably right." He squinted at the door. "I just have to find someone desperate enough to give up her life for a chance at immortality. And strong enough to survive the sealing and the birth of my child. Shouldn't be all that hard." Put that way, it felt seductively easy. But Leonidas was completely uneducated in matters of love and knew he had absolutely no idea what he was talking about. He slid his smirk back to his brother, but Lucian's face had gone serious again.

"My greatest fear is that you'll lose your heart. You know that, right?"

Leonidas swallowed and just nodded. He was the youngest brother, only two minutes behind first-born Lucian, but Lucian already had two great loves in his life— Leonidas was an infant by comparison.

"I'm no help to you there," Lucian said. "But I think the key is to just treat this as the dutiful business that it is. Seduction is something you do well—have faith in that. Know that you can make this happen without losing your way. And I stand by your right side at all times."

The lump in Leonidas's throat just grew. "If your intent is to make me into an emotional wreck, my brother, you're managing it quite well."

That worked a smile back on Lucian's face. "So I take it the first two candidates were unacceptable."

"One was as weak and foul tempered as a dishrag,"

Leonidas said, his lip curling in disgust. "The other was fantastically beautiful, truly a work of womanly art."

"But?" Amusement was alive on Lucian's face.

"But she was spoiled beyond belief, and that's *before* she's an actual princess of the House of Smoke." Leonidas dropped his chin and raised his eyebrow. "I require someone who has been thoroughly neglected in order to properly pamper her myself."

Lucian squeezed his eyes shut and just shook his head. When he opened them, his smirk grew stronger. "Sounds like you have this under control."

Leonidas gestured to the door. "What I don't understand is how you got so many women to the keep on such short notice."

"WildLove." Lucian's eyes sparkled.

Leonidas frowned. "Pardon?"

"WildLove, the app," Lucian explained. "The one that hooks up humans and shifters. We posted—Arabella and I —that you were a shifter in great need of a mate, immediately. Only women who wanted a lifelong commitment should apply."

Leonidas had heard of the app, of course, but he preferred to frequent the shifter bars in downtown Seattle. Unfortunately, the women tended to be looking for a one-night affair. "So that worked?"

"We added in the part about you being desperate."

Leonidas scowled but was barely holding back his laughter. "Well, all of that is completely true."

Lucian squeezed his shoulder and released him. "This is just the first round, Leonidas. There are plenty more fish in that ocean if these aren't to your liking."

"My liking has very little relevance to the subject at hand." Leonidas straightened his shoulders. "This is purely business, right?"

Lucian tried to hide the flash of sadness that whisked across his face… but Leonidas saw it. "Right."

"Then let's get to it." Leonidas pulled in a breath and stalked toward the door. He opened it and gestured his brother to go through first. Leksander was already out in the room, prescreening the women and making sure they understood the terms of the arrangement. No spilling the secret location of the keep, should they actually discern it. No revealing that the House was filled with dragon shifters, not the usual wolfish kind. And Leksander was making sure they understood the concept of mating—that it was a life-long affair, sealed in magic, not to be broken by any human accords. All of that was nothing really, barely a glimpse of what they were signing up for. The truly horrific parts would be revealed later, and only to those who made the final cut.

Lucian went ahead of Leonidas into the throne room where the women gathered. He drew their attention with his regal medieval attire, complete with black trousers under a golden tunic blazed with the dragon crest of their House. The power of his walk assured them he was the sovereign in charge, and Leonidas had no doubt he could have any of them in a heartbeat, were his heart not already lost to Arabella and little Larik.

Leonidas had dressed more casually, donning his regular seduction uniform, a modern club-going outfit of black pants with a tailored black silk shirt. He was well aware of how it set off his muscular dragon form—that, plus the pheromones his kind exuded in abundance, were usually more than enough to make human women hot and ready.

It was more or less a science and a simple one.

Inducing *lust* was well within his purview; it was the *love* part of the equation that would challenge him. Fortunately,

Leonidas and his brothers were part of the royal line descended from the original pairing of a dragon and the Queen of the Summer Fae Court that resulted in the treaty to begin with. The blood in his veins was a blessing and a curse, but it gave him the ability to taste the women assembled before him in more ways than one.

The attention of the room had finally shifted from Lucian to him as he stood on the threshold of his receiving room, scanning the two dozen or more lovely human females. It was a slightly better-looking crowd than he would find in Seattle's openly-shifter bars, where humans and shifters came to have hot, anonymous couplings. He realized with a jolt that his days of having whichever female he pleased, three or more in a night if that was his yearning, were well and truly behind him. Whoever he mated with, he would be bound to for life. There could be no second-guessing, no infidelities, nothing that would jeopardize the True Love that was necessary to make the sealing and the carrying of his dragonling a success.

He would have to put on a Shakespearean-level performance, a fantastically rendered simulacrum of epic love. One that would make this female, whichever he chose, fall heedlessly in love with him, willing to risk life and heart to his embrace.

It was a cruel act. He knew it, but she never could.

On pain of death, he couldn't allow himself to fall in love with her in return but, by all that was magic, he could at least pick a beauty. And one that was capable in bed, although he could tutor just about any woman in the arts of love—he had certainly proved that in the past. But if he was going to force himself to share the bed of only one woman for the next five hundred years, he would at least give himself the gift of a beautiful one. One whose thoughts wouldn't matter while she was moaning and screaming under him.

He was stalling.

A hush had fallen over the crowd as the women waited for him to pick the next for interview. A scuffle and a raised voice at the back of the room drew his attention, along with everyone else.

"I'm sorry," his brother, Leksander, was saying to a woman near the door. They were a good thirty feet away, but Leonidas could easily see the look of righteous anger on the woman's face. The power of it somehow made her more beautiful, but she was already stunning. Flame-red hair in long, flowing waves that fell nearly to her pertly rounded bottom. Porcelain skin that glowed even across the room. Blazing blue eyes that were trained on his brother's. Leksander's hulking, muscular dragon form stood several inches taller than her, even in her spiky black heels. She stood defiantly in her slinky, curve-hugging black dress, and those curves… Leonidas was already picturing her in his bed. And definitely approving.

"You have no right!" the woman said. Although she was barely more than a girl, early twenties at the oldest. She jabbed a finger into Leksander's chest, and he gave her a look like she had crossed some indefinable line of insult. Of course, his brother would never hurt a female, least of all a human one. Dragons were protectors of the human realm, by treaty and by instinct. But this spunky, beautiful girl was insulting his authority.

And if she kept going, Leksander just might throw her out.

His brother seemed suddenly aware of all the attention on them and threw a furtive glance at Leonidas, but avoided meeting his gaze.

Leksander lowered his voice, but it still carried. "I'm

sorry, but you have to leave. The prince doesn't have time to meet with everyone today."

Leonidas frowned. Why was his brother trying to get rid of this woman? He reached out with his fae senses, the ones that allowed him to taste the essence of a person. The fundamental nature and defining experiences left an imprint he could sense, up to and including their sexual history. He used it every night to do his own prescreening to find which willing woman had the most experience in bed and would provide the most lively and pleasurable entertainment for them both. He'd tasted every type of woman there was to taste… but his quick sampling of the red-haired beauty standing at his brother's side jolted him.

A witch.

Holy fucking magic, *a witch* had answered the post for his Mating Game?

Before Leonidas even realized what he was doing, he was striding the length of the throne room, brushing past the gap-mouthed faces of the women who'd been standing and waiting patiently. He ignored their looks of concern and curiosity and slight affront in his determination to reach the back of the room before Leksander threw this little witch out of their keep.

Lucian met him halfway, but Leonidas didn't slow down. "What are you doing?" Lucian asked, voice hushed.

Leonidas didn't even look at him. "Just business, right?" His heart was thrumming. *A witch* had cursed him. A witch was responsible for the hundreds of years during which he was denied the ability to ever fall in love. She'd stolen a fundamental part of his soul, his life, using deep and ancient magic in a way that no one else, short of a fae, could. *A witch* was responsible for the very predicament he found himself in, and a witch would be the perfect one to fix it.

The perfect mate.

Because he may not know much of love, but he knew one thing for certain—he would never fall in love with a witch.

Leksander was hurriedly entreating the woman. "Please. You must go. This isn't—" He cut off with Leonidas's glare.

Then he turned the full brilliance of his most seductive smile on the witch. "Please excuse my brother. He left his manners back in the sixteenth century." He reached his hand out to shake hers. "I'm Leonidas Smoke, Prince of the House of Smoke. And I am ever so pleased to meet you."

Her eyes went wide, blue and brilliant and still enlivened by the anger she had been directing at Leksander. She quickly recovered and reached out to shake.

"I'm Rosalyn Thorne, and I'm pleased—" She cut off and jerked slightly when they touched, surprised by the spark that flew between her hand and his.

Oh yes. She might be surprised, but Leonidas knew exactly what that pleasure-inducing magical blue spark was... and what it portended for when she lay writhing under him in his bed. Her eyes went even wider, but her hand stayed in his. He drew it closer and brushed his lips across the back of her fingers, sparking even more pleasure as he painted magic across her skin. He kept his moan inside, but his cock was already responding to her touch and all its promise.

Her mouth dropped open, and her eyes fell to half-mast with the pleasure.

He released her hand before they went too much further—otherwise, his arousal would be far too obvious in a room filled with other women and his two brothers.

"I… am…" She was struggling for words, and Leonidas had to rein in his smirk.

She was the perfect choice.

Leksander's face was afire with disapproval, and he was making some kind of chopping gesture with his hand behind Rosalyn's back. Lucian's glare was two shades darker than before.

"If you'll excuse us," Leonidas said lightly to his brothers, sweeping a hand toward the interview room. "Ms. Thorne and I have an appointment."

Leksander looked like he was going to choke on his own spit. Lucian's jaw worked, but no words came out. Rosalyn tipped her head, accepting Leonidas's invitation, and walked ahead of him. He trailed behind, careful not to touch her again. He'd already laid out the bait. She would take it soon enough.

He could feel his brothers' heated stares on his back, and he knew just what they were thinking—there couldn't be a more disastrous choice for a mate than a witch. That somehow this might spell Leonidas's doom, given the curse that lay heavily on him for centuries. But they weren't the ones who had lived with it, ruminated on it, reviled and railed against it… and eventually, made his peace with it. They weren't the ones who were doomed to never fall in love. Lucian had done it twice, deeply. Leksander was slavishly in love with an angeling he could never have, presenting his own difficulties in fulfilling the treaty.

But Leonidas?

He had never loved a witch… *and he never would.*

Chapter Two

Everything Rosalyn had heard about shifters being *hot* was spot on.

She put a little sway in her step as she strode into the "interview room" with tall, dark, and ridiculously handsome behind her. She pretended to check out the sparse accommodations of the small room while she waited for him to follow her inside and then close the door. She half expected to see a "casting couch" in here, given the flustered faces of the two women who had hurriedly left after their brief encounter with this shifter Prince of Whatever. Maybe he just touched them with that sparking thing that jumped from his hand to hers.

What the hell was *that?*

An involuntary shudder of remembered pleasure rippled through her. *Get it together, Rose,* she scolded herself, forcing an alluring smile as she turned to face the dangerously sexy man leaning against the door. His arms were crossed, and he was checking her out.

A flush of heat chased that shiver, her body responding to the hunger in his eyes. He was obviously hot for her, and her body was acting like jumping him was the next obvious step. *Fuck.* She knew shifters were hot, but she didn't expect this full-body, visceral response, much less whatever that magic sparking thing was between them. In theory, physical attraction should make her job here easier, but in actuality, the last thing she wanted was to *respond* to this powerful man's overwhelming sex appeal. She couldn't afford to lose control like that, and she had *zero* interest in actually fucking him.

Despite what her body was trying to tell her.

She put a little more flirt into her smile. "So, how does this work?"

He bit his lip in a way that seemed entirely intentional, but it still sent another one of those rippling shudders of pleasure through her. *For the love of magic...* she tried desperately to calm her body's seemingly automatic response. Sure, he was gorgeous. Dark, slightly reddish-tinted hair. Dazzling, sapphire-blue eyes alive with intelligence. A chiseled jaw and high, carved cheekbones, making him just a little too rough to be an actual pretty boy. And that body... it was like he'd stepped out of a men's fitness magazine and dressed up to go clubbing. *A shifter who seduced women.* She's never met one before, but she knew all she needed about men like him. And this guy was exactly how she imagined—top-drawer sexy, full of himself, and ready to jump in her pants.

He was taking his time in answering. "First, we talk," he said with a growing smirk. "Right now, I'm testing to see who I'm sexually compatible with."

Of course. Forget the casting couch—he could just take her right on the floor or bend her over one of the stuffed chairs.

She crossed her arms and cocked her hip to one side. "So, you're just fucking a bunch of women?" She put acid in her voice. She would not get what she wanted if this was all a charade, and he just screwed her and sent her on her way. "You're not serious about this mating thing." She dropped a heavy dose of accusation into her voice.

His smile faltered, just a little, but she saw it. She kept in her own smirk.

"No, I'm serious about that. Deadly serious."

She raised an eyebrow and eased one step closer, letting her arms unlock and her body open a little. She had curves that men had a hard time ignoring, and she knew how to use them. Not that she actually dated—men were fine for some sexual relief every once in a while, but more than that, and they were just trouble. *Especially* the non-human kind. With everything she and her mom had been through, it was clear that men just fucked things up. Life was simpler and frankly better when it was just her, her mom, and her shop of magical artifacts. But she understood how men worked, and she could haggle with the best. They came and went from her shop, peddling their powders and potions and illegally obtained body parts, and she could easily charm them down from their ridiculously overpriced starting offers. Especially when she undid a button or two on her blouse.

Whatever it took to seal the deal. Just like here.

"So what's our next step, then?" she asked. "I signed that extensive non-disclosure agreement your fellow prince-brother or whatever foisted upon me. I'd thought you were just another wolf, but the fact that you're a *dragon* shifter doesn't bother me. I'm assuming there's not some kind of weird, hidden feature to that." In truth, the fact he was a dragon made this all the more alluring. It was a stroke of luck, and she took those seriously, considering most of her luck had been of the *bad* variety. She'd thought dragons were just a myth, but if half the stories were true…

He frowned, just a little, but his eyes were still sparkling. He unlocked his arms and moved away from the door, stepping a little closer. There were still several feet between them. Rosalyn hoped she could close this deal without having to get any closer. Any more of that electric-sparking touch, and she might be the one pulling him down to the floor. And that definitely wouldn't get her what she needed. Which, she reminded her body, *wasn't* an orgasm. Especially not with this man—*this shifter*. Fuck no. No matter how hot he was.

"What kind of strange feature were you thinking?" he asked, a little too curious.

She cocked her hip again, planting a fist on it and giving her patented, steely-eyed negotiating stare. And absolutely no lust. None. "Well, Leo… can I call you Leo?"

"My name is Leonidas, and I'm a prince of the House of Smoke." His smirk was almost a laugh. "You can call me anything you like."

Oh God. "Okay, Mr. Smoke, is there something I should know about this dragon business? Are you going to erupt into a fiery blast of magic when we're in the middle of the act? That seems like something I should know ahead of time." She had no intention of going that far, but she wanted him to think she was willing in the sex department. Which she definitely was not.

His sultry smirk dissolved into a snorting laugh. "No. Nothing like that."

"No slicing talons that come out when you're bouncing the bed? No uncontrolled shifting and shredding of sheets?" She gave him a little smile.

He stepped closer. "Well, maybe we should give it a try and find out…"

She moved back and put up her hands. "Slow down, hot stuff. I'm still getting my bearings."

He stopped his advance but smiled, and it almost seemed genuine—not that flirty little thing he'd been throwing at her or the steamy looks that felt like raw heat across her skin. This was just pure enjoyment, and it wormed its way into her. She steeled herself against it—even if this Leonidas character was some kind of nice guy and not a spoiled dragon prince looking to be the ultimate prize in his own Bachelor Game, that meant nothing. He was still a shifter. She was after one thing and one thing only—*his blood.*

And everything it would unlock for her.

"I'll let you set the pace, then," he said, quietly, his voice unexpectedly tender. "But I can already tell there's something special about you." He lifted his hand, the one they used to shake with, and rubbed his thumb along each of his fingertips in turn—a movement so slow and erotic that heat made a mad-dash for that space between her legs that insisted it had been lonely way too long. And his fingers were long. *So long. Oh God.* What those hands would do to her...

Fuck. *He's a goddamn shifter!* she reminded herself. *You are not doing this with him.*

Not unless and until absolutely necessary. And then she would get the hell out.

Rosalyn straightened her shoulders and lifted her chin. "Good. I don't know what you have in mind with this whole charade." She swept her hand toward the door and the women beyond. He could have any of them—*she didn't care*—once she was done with him. But for now, he needed to think she was the only one worth noticing. That she was the pick of the lot, desperately seeking forever-love and hot sex, even if she was nothing of the sort. She would lure him into her trap, and once she got what she needed, she would let him go. *Catch and release.* Just like every other man she'd ever been with, only this one wouldn't be giving her a few quick orgasms before heading on his way.

He would give her something much more valuable.

"This isn't a charade," he said, frowning. "I'm very serious about finding just the right woman to be my mate and bear my dragonling." And he was, deadly serious, all of a sudden.

"Dragonling? As in… baby dragon?" There were no babies mentioned in the WildLove post… then again, she supposed that came with the whole *mating* thing.

"Very much so." He still smoldered with seriousness. "I'm a prince—I need to carry on the line. The role of princess of the House of Smoke isn't one that just any woman can shoulder. It can be a burden. There are parts that are… difficult. I'm not simply looking for someone to heat my bed, Rosalyn." He took a step closer, and that smoldering look was warming her skin again. "I need a strong woman who can go the distance with me. A partner by my side. Someone who will have my child and spend the next five hundred years with me."

"Sounds like a very serious decision." She desperately tried to ignore the tremor running races through her body, but it was hardening her nipples underneath her skimpy black dress.

And Leonidas was definitely noticing.

He licked his lips. "Very serious."

"Then you'll understand, I hope," she said, easing back a little, "that I might need a bit of time to decide if this is the right thing for me. *For us,*" she added, trying to make it sound like she wasn't hesitating. Just prudent. Logical. Not at all trying to lure him out of this keep where he was far too protected and had too many fellow dragons ready to come to his aid.

The heat in his eyes cooled. "Time is something I don't have much of."

She frowned. There was more than a touch of real morbidness in that. As if he were about to die of cancer or something. *Fuck.* She really hoped it wasn't something like that. Did dragons get cancer? Would it affect his blood? That didn't make sense, but crap, she knew nothing about dragons. Not really. Who did?

If he was sick, that might very much ruin her plans, not least because stealing blood from a dying man… even *she* wasn't prepared to do that. Not if he was actually dying.

"What do you mean by that?" she asked, searching his face for some tell about this. Was he lying? Was it a sympathy bid? He flinched a little, and that was a bad sign. Whatever he was about to say was *true.* More than that… it was *costing* him something to reveal it. If he would even say it…

Her throat tightened. This whole thing might be screwed already.

He frowned. "It's a dragon thing, but you've already signed the non-disclosure, so…" He dropped his gaze to the polished granite floor. "This isn't something I planned on telling you so soon." He peered up. *Holy magic,* his lashes were long and dark, and the way his brilliant blue eyes glittered through them… "Maybe we should save that part for later. I don't want to scare you off."

"No, we're definitely *not* saving it for later." Her voice hiked up. If this was blowing everything for her, trashing all her plans even before she got out of the gate… she cleared her throat and tried to soften her voice. At least *sound* sympathetic, Rose. For fuck's sake, the man was dying. Or something. "This is mating we're talking about, right? I just came in here because I was curious about the whole thing," she said, trotting out her cover story. "With shifters being in the headlines, all persecuted and everything—by the way, I *never* thought that was right—I've read up, done my homework, and everything I've seen makes me think a shifter might be just the kind of man I've been looking for my whole life."

"Really?" He frowned, just a little. Like she was some kind of puzzle he was figuring out.

"Yeah, really," she rushed out. "I mean, I don't know if dragon shifters are anything like wolves, but the whole idea of a man who knows what he wants, who mates for life, magically bound to love and protect, and who's hotter than sin in bed..." She arched an eyebrow, and the smirk was quickly back on his face. "Let's just say human men don't measure up. Especially not the ones I've dated." Well, that much was true. Not that she thought shifters were *all that*— she knew too well how a hot shifter could destroy everything that mattered. One had done exactly that to her mother, taking Rosalyn down in the fallout, and it was only right that a shifter could pay a little blood to make it right again.

As long as he wasn't *dying*.

He took a half step closer, his eyes glittering again. "So the men in your life haven't measured up?"

That was certainly true. "Maybe my standards are too high."

"I doubt that," he said, dropping his voice into something soft and seductive. "You're the kind of woman who deserves the best of everything."

Ugh. He thought she was some kind of arrogant... "Look," she said, stepping back from the personal space he seemed to be trying to step into. "I just need to know the truth before we get too far with this." She peered up into his eyes. "What is this business about you not having much time? Because if you're dying or something… *that changes things.*"

His eyes went wide.

She held up her hands. "Not saying it's a deal-breaker, but…" She threw a pinched look at the door. What was really going on here? Was this a version of speed-dating for a dying shifter prince so he could pass on his crown or something? She looked back at him, and there was an almost comical look of struggle on his face, as if he wanted to say something but couldn't find the words to save his soul. It reached inside her again, and she tried to seal her heart against it, but she couldn't—she was tough, but not made of granite. "Look, I won't tell anyone," she said, softening her voice as well. "If this is all just so you can make a baby before you, you know, *run out of time,* then okay. I can see that. I'm just… I'm not the woman for that job." *Shit.* She was throwing away her chance for some Grade A dragon blood here, but if the guy didn't have time—or blood—to spare, she didn't want to be the one to steal away his last chance at leaving a legacy behind.

He was just shaking his head and blinking. Which was damn strange.

"You're shaking your head *no,*" she said, impatience crawling up her neck. "No to which part?"

A small smile grew on his face. "No, I… I'm just a little surprised, is all."

"About what? Exactly." *Fuck,* she should just bail out of this entirely. She flicked a look at the door, but she'd have to shove past his all-too-hot body to get there.

"Surprised that you… *care.*" He was drilling a look into her now like he wanted to pierce her soul with those blazing-blue eyes.

What? "Okay, I'm out of here." She nearly went down

with her spiky black heels—what the hell was she thinking wearing those? Oh right, that she would lure some shifter asshole into giving up his blood—

He caught her arm as she passed—just a gentle squeeze, then he let go. Not enough to stop her, and that crazy electricity zapping thing didn't seem to work through the sleeve of her dress, but she still screeched to a standstill. Mostly to give him a piece of her mind. "You know what? Even if you're dying, you don't have to—"

"Rosalyn, *please.*" The desperation in his voice stopped her cold.

She just blinked.

"Just let me explain, okay?" he asked, and it was soft. Painful. Tender.

Oh shit. He was going to try to sell her on something— she could feel it. And yet, her heels were planted on the granite floor, not running for the door, like she should be.

"I'm five hundred years old, Rosalyn."

Her eyes widened with surprise, but she kept her mouth shut. *Was this for real?* And *holy magic,* if his blood kept him alive that long...

"And that's not the only way dragon shifters are different," he continued, voice still soft. "At the end of our lives, we turn into... well, we call it a wyvern form, but basically, it's our own personal Beast Mode. When my time is up, I'll become a mindless, dangerous, incredibly powerful dragon beast that pretty much has to be put down for the safety of everyone."

"Holy shit," she said, not entirely sure she believed him, but why lie about that? "That's... pretty awful."

His smile was back, and it relaxed her somehow. "Yeah. It is. And my time is just about up, but there's an escape clause, of sorts. If I can find a mate—a true mate, someone who can actually love me—and spawn a dragonling with her, then the magic somehow renews for another five hundred years. Time to raise a dragonling and watch over him, I suppose. I don't know why it works that way, but it does."

She was shaking her head a little. This was crazy. But the old stories—the ones she heard at her mother's knee instead of the spells a witch *ought* to teach her daughter—hinted that dragons were practically immortal. And this fit that bill. Plus this Prince Leonidas person seemed entirely sincere. It could all be a con... but in the magical world, she knew many things were possible that seemed bat-shit crazy.

"So, you'll die if you don't mate and produce a drag-onling," she said, carefully. "But if you *do* mate and make a baby, then all's good for another five hundred years."

"Exactly." That sexy smile was back again. "It can't be just anyone, though. It has to be someone... *magical.*"

She couldn't help the grin that wrenched out of her. "Magical."

"Yes." His smoldering hotness was back full-force.

Rosalyn's smile grew. Because if Prince Hot Stuff wasn't *actually* dying, then the game was back on—and he could spare a little blood before finding his magical mate to make babies and live with forever. "Well, then. We should do this right."

"And how would that be?" he asked, eyes alight with curiosity again.

Gotcha, Dragon Prince. "I have a little shop. Magical arti-facts—I'm a dealer."

His eyes narrowed. "So you're a witch."

Her heart lurched. *Oh, crap.* Witches and shifters were sworn enemies—no way was she letting that slip. "No, no, I'm just a dealer. I mean, I do business with the covens, supply them with their potions and things, but everyone has to make a living, right? You can't hold that against me."

He frowned, and her heart kept knocking around in her chest. But getting him to the shop was key, so she'd better step this up a notch. She gestured to his fancy, magical keep all around them—it was tucked in the mountains, draped in finery and glass and all kinds of expensive shit. She'd gaped at the place just like the rest of the parade of women answering the WildLove post. "Maybe billionaire dragon shifters don't have to make a living, but common folk like myself do."

His smile was back, although it was mixed around with that frown. "You're far from common, Rosalyn."

"Well, you're not so bad, yourself," she said, internally cringing because *holy magic* she was genuinely bad at flirting. Saucily teasing customers? Sure. But actually engaging in sexy talk? With a gorgeous hunk of man like Leonidas Smoke? Not so much. *"Anyway…"* She cleared her throat. Yeah, not awkward at all. "Between the business and taking care of my mom, that's pretty much my whole life. Maybe we can't do the whole dating thing—you know, like normal people—but if you want to know if I'm the kind of woman who could be your true mate, there's no better way than to come visit my shop. Maybe spend a little time together. You know, talking. And things."

"And things." He smirked.

She narrowed her eyes. "Not *that* thing. Well… maybe that thing. But only if you're serious. About the mating, I mean. I don't want to, shall we say, get in too deep, if this isn't going to work out."

"You're not the kind for one night stands," he said, eyes alight again. "You want it for real. For life."

"Exactly." Which wasn't even close to true, but that

didn't matter. On the inside, she was doing a small victory dance. He'd taken the bait—hook, line, and sinker.

"Then I'd better come visit your shop." His smile was wide now, beaming and full of promise. He was so damn sexy, it was a shame she wasn't going to take him to bed. Or see him any time after his visit to her shop/home/care-fully-planned-opportunity-to-extract-dragon-blood. His long fingers tapped her address and number into his phone, then she hurried her ass out of there before anything else could go sideways.

Trap: successfully set.

Now she just had to wait for him to walk into it.

Chapter Three

Leonidas had a date. *With a witch.*

A rush of excitement had been filling his body ever since Rosalyn strode out of the interview room, that long red hair bouncing on her back, her hips swaying, oh so deliciously. She left without a look back, but if she had, she would've caught him staring and fighting to keep from sporting an erection right there in the middle of the throne room.

Damn, she was hot. And feisty. The sex with her would be fantastic.

Over his brothers' objections, Leonidas told them to clear the room and dismiss the rest of the women. Then he hurried off to his lair to shower and change and get ready for his date. He was actually anticipating it, which made him chuckle lightly as he was getting a fresh shave and towel drying his hair. It would take her time to drive back to Seattle, to the little magical artifacts shop she apparently ran, but he wanted to be there when she arrived. It was easy enough to fly ahead of her—the difficulty would be getting his brothers to let him out of the keep.

Actually, his biggest challenge would be convincing this feisty little witch to fall in love with him, but he was certain that once he got her into his bed, the delights she would find there—not just his five hundred years' worth of skills in pleasing women, but that extra, sizzling magical touch due to her being a witch—surely would have her falling for him. Eventually.

Just in case, he wanted to look a little into her background. She was young, but everyone had something in their past. He could taste her sexual experience, and it wasn't insubstantial—not a surprise, given how hot and hotheaded and hard-driving she was. But there was darkness there as well, buried under the bravado. He needed to figure out what it was. But it clearly hadn't slowed her down in the slightest.

This was a woman who took what she wanted.

And Leonidas was determined to be *exactly* what she wanted.

But first, he had to convince his brothers of the perfection of his plan… and that his wyvern wasn't taking over and driving him into crazy acts, like trying to mate with a witch.

He checked himself in the mirror—just a casual t-shirt and jeans. They fit well and showed off the features he knew made women want to get up close and personal with him, although he could usually rely on dragon pheromones to do most of the heavy lifting. He hoped the slightly more down-to-earth approach would have the intended effect— he could already tell she had a finely-tuned bullshit meter. Pretentiousness crawled under her skin.

He squinted at the mirror. "What happened to this little witch to make her loathe someone with the trappings of power?" he asked his reflection. "Yet seek out a billion-aire shifter to mate with?" The puzzle of her intrigued him just as much as that highly anticipated first time they would spend in bed.

He frowned, hesitant for a moment. Was his attempt to look "normal" too obvious? Would she see right through it? She already had an unsettling ability to see straight to the heart of the matter—he was dying. She had picked up on that when the others hadn't, and she seemed to respond best when he was telling the truth. He knew women were like that—they wanted you to open your heart and soul to them.

He frowned harder. *That* was something he guarded hard against. And he couldn't start slipping up now.

He gave his reflection a sharp nod. "Right. No fucking around, except in bed," he chastised himself, then turned away to stride toward the door.

A quick glance around his lair on the way out convinced him that returning here was not the best choice. He liked his place neat and upscale. The white carpet and couches, the bronze motif of ancient urns and beaten metal art on the wall—all of it screamed *money*. And probably pretentiousness. His first time with Rosalyn needed to be somewhere else, perhaps on her own turf. Or something wild and daring—maybe a public place.

He ticked through the catalog of thousands of couplings he'd had over his lifetime—there was a lot to choose from. He would just have to be on the lookout for the right time and place for Ms. Rosalyn Thorne.

As he contemplated the best way to bed a witch, he strode across the keep toward the throne room and hoped his brothers had cleared the place out. Lucky for him, by the time he arrived, only the two of them remained. Unfortunately, they were no less pissed than when he left.

Leksander was busy magicking away the chairs the women had been sitting on, but he whirled on Leonidas when he saw him, stomping fast across the span of the throne room. "What the fuck are you doing?"

Leonidas braced for a fight, planting his feet wide and staring down Leksander. "I know exactly—"

"Oh, for fuck's sake," Lucian cut him off, striding over as well. "You have no idea what you're doing."

Leonidas glared at him. "Meaning what, exactly?"

Leksander checked his pace just before reaching Leonidas, but his fist was up and ready.

Leonidas glared at him. "Really? Are we going to do this, my brother?"

Leksander turned away and let out a bellow, along with a swiping gust of dragonfire. It vented his anger across the throne room with a long roar. The draperies smoldered, but Leksander dropped his fist and shook it out.

"Nice," Leonidas said with a sneer. "And you're worried about *me* losing my mind. Wait till mother sees this."

Leksander just turned a slow glare on him. "Don't fuck this up, Leonidas," he ground out.

Lucian let out a long sigh and stepped forward until he was right in front of Leonidas. "A witch?" Lucian asked. "Really?"

Great. So much for Lucian's support.

Leonidas held up his hands. "Well, now that you're asking nicely, perhaps I could explain why this is my most brilliant idea ever."

Lucian gave him a pinched look, and Leksander just shook his head like he was hopeless, but at least they weren't throwing dragonfire at him. Anymore.

"Yes, a witch gave me my curse," Leonidas said, calmly. "And yes, I am taking this deadly seriously." He slid a dark look to Leksander who was still glowering. "But if you two scales-for-brains would just think clearly about this for a second, you would see the utter brilliance of it."

Lucian looked faintly amused. "Do enlighten us. Quickly. I can probably still catch the majority of those women before they leave the keep."

Leonidas hooked a thumb over his shoulder, gesturing toward the throne room door. "Those women… did you bother tasting them? Because I did. They're weak, Lucian. The first ones who jumped on an ad to marry a billionaire dragon shifter? I'm sure they're a bunch of really nice, sweet women—and some of them were pretty hot—but that's not really our criteria here, now is it? We need someone who can carry a dragonling. And Rosalyn is *a witch.* She's already a magical creature. And did you get a sense of her? She's fucking powerful. Totally not fessing up to that at the moment—I'm working on that part—but she was hands-down the best candidate in the room with just that fact alone."

"None of that will mean anything," Leksander ground out, "if you can't convince her to love you. Or—and this is a hell of a lot more likely—she fucks with your head. If you turn wyvern, Leonidas, it's game over. *We're done.*" Literal dragonfire was leaking from the corners of his mouth. Leonidas had never seen him so worked up. He was usually the cooler, more levelheaded, of the three of them. Lucian had dark and brooding covered most of the time, although since he mated with Arabella and had his son Larik, he was like a new man, all sunshine and smiles… until the shit hit the fan again. Leonidas was mainly comic relief. So he could see why they didn't take him seriously.

But that had to stop *now.*

"Don't you see how perfect it is?" he asked. "A witch cursed me to never love another woman. So, naturally, I'm not a fan of witches. The danger of me falling in love with this particular woman—*who is also a witch*—is infinitesimally small."

Lucian was studying him, almost like he was taking Leonidas's words seriously for a change. "If you hate witches so much, how are you going to get this one to fall in love with you?"

Leonidas threw up his hands. "I lie to women *all the time.*" He dropped them for emphasis as if that should be obvious. "What the fuck do you think I've been doing for five hundred years? Lying to women, getting them in my bed, and then having to break their hearts once they fell in love. Been 'round this rodeo, Lucian. I'm not an amateur here."

His brother cocked an eyebrow. "That's a different tune than you were singing just before Rosalyn walked in the door."

Leonidas tipped his head in acknowledgment. No sense in denying the obvious. "Granted, I had a moment of self-doubt. But that's passed." Then he stared his brother in the eyes. "Lucian, I've watched you and Arabella fall in love, and I will admit that caused me no small amount of pain. Call it jealousy. Call it once again remembering that's not something I'll ever have. *Whatever.* You don't get the corner market on moody, all right? But you *are* right about what you said, back there in the interview room—women fall in love with me all the time. And I *don't* fall in love with them, now do I? It was the prospect of facing five hundred years with just *one* of them that was making me go a little crazy in the head. Because how is that going to turn out? Let's just imagine that for a moment, shall we? Say I successfully seduce a woman into loving me and bearing my child. I see how you look at Larik. I see what it does to your heart. How it softens. What do you think will happen once I have a dragonling of my own? How do you think I'll feel about his mother?"

Lucian was nodding now, and he had to see it—Leonidas would be lucky to guard his heart against falling in love with the woman carrying his child all the way through to the end of the pregnancy. But once the baby was born? He would be done for.

"So what are you saying?" Leksander asked with a pinched look, like he was finally coming back to his senses, and the rational part of his brain was kicking in. "That you're guaranteed not to fall in love with this Rosalyn, even after the baby is born, because she's a witch?"

Leonidas raised his hands to the heavens. "Now he gets it." Then he looked to Lucian. "You know what mated sex is like. It's the same with a witch *before* mating. I can't even imagine what it will be like after. I'll have real and solid reasons to hate her kind, and to *not* fall in love with her specifically, but if I manage to stay out of the danger zone, that extra magical spark will compensate for having to spend the rest of my life with a woman I can never love."

Leonidas was playing a little dirty with that last part—he knew it broke Lucian's heart that Leonidas was cursed to never have what he had with Arabella. Hell, it broke Leonidas's heart too.

"At this point," Leonidas said, "the only thing that matters is the treaty. You both need to just back off and stay out of my way until I get this taken care of."

Lucian nodded and looked to Leksander. He was back to looking pensive, a lot more like his normal state. There was a long pause, but Leksander finally gave him a nod.

Leonidas clasped his hands together and gave his brother a bow. "Thank you." Then he turned toward the door to get moving on that promise, but before he got two steps, the door flew open—and a beautiful woman stormed through it.

Not a woman—an angeling. *Erelah.*

She was unearthly beautiful, just like all the angels and their half-angel, half-human offspring, the angelings. Her long blonde hair flowed behind her, and she barely had any clothes to cover that voluptuous, feminine form that drove his brother Leksander to distraction. But it was the fiery look in her eyes that caught everyone's attention, all lit up with passion and fervor like she was fresh off a demon kill. That was eye-catching, along with the angel blade she still had gripped in her hand, swinging at her side. Leonidas reflexively stepped back, but she wasn't headed for him anyway.

Her perky breasts bounced as she quickly strode up to Leksander and said, breathlessly, "We found a whole nest of them!"

"The demon-infected ones?" Leksander asked, clearly happy to see her, but still giving a wary eye to the knife. Given it was one of the few things which could pierce dragon skin, and angelings weren't known for their calm demeanor, a little caution was in order.

"Yes!" she cried, gripping the knife tighter. "Markos is helping me find them!" At the mention of the True Angel's name, Leksander's initial happy expression fell into a dark scowl. Supposedly, angels never took angelings to bed— something about it being *verboten* in the angel world—but his brother was so far gone in love with Erelah that it hardly mattered. He'd be jealous of the lamppost she leaned against.

And now, with the treaty pressing him to find a mate…

"I would've helped you." Leksander gestured to the now-cleared throne room. "In fact, we're done here. I can go to Seattle with you now and help." They'd spent the last week hunting for the demon-infected humans that had somehow broke into the keep and staged the attack under Tytus's direction.

It was still a mystery how he had summoned a demon mercenary force that could slip past their magical wards, not to mention what the ramifications of that were for the human realm. The House of Smoke was supposed to be protecting the humans, watching over them. Not simply because dragons needed humans for mating, nor simply because of the treaty, which kept the peace. Dragons and angels had common cause in a genuine love of the soft, mortal creatures in their care, although the angels and their angelings had the corner market on the *crazy love* aspect of that.

Leksander and Erelah had been scouring the streets of Seattle, trying to ensure the general population was safe and searching for more demons, but they'd mostly come up empty. Occasionally, they would find a hapless demon-infected human that Erelah stabbed with her angel blade, liberating the demon from its human host. But that didn't answer where the demon mercenaries had come from or how they were made.

"You said you found a nest of them," Lucian said, stepping into this. "How many?"

Erelah turned to him, her face lighting up again. It was as if Leksander had ceased to exist. "Only five—an entire family. But I thought I should tell you, in case you wished to question them before I destroyed the demons possessing them."

She raised her blade and shook it, and that fervent warrior angel passion radiated from her. She was sexy as hell when she did that, and Leonidas could understand the effect it had on his brother, but Leksander's need for her went far, far beyond that. He'd loved Erelah for decades now, nearly the full century since she'd been created, always unrequited. Angelings were only interested in humans—in fact, the thing True Angels had for humans was more than a little unseemly. Their desire to love upon God's creations, as the angels saw them, was a little too fervent… but angels and angelings alike had no interest in dragons.

In modern times, dragons and angelings hardly had cause to cross paths at all. Demons hadn't roamed the earth for hundreds of years, not with the successful wiping out the remnants left over from the ten-thousand-year-old treaty. Preventing the fae from conjuring more demons to torment humanity was just one of the many reasons Leonidas was working hard to renew the treaty. But now that demons were popping up all over Seattle, for reasons they'd yet to decipher, angelings like Erelah were in a righteous ecstasy of destruction. Even angels like Markos were helping, which was a wonder, given they were forbidden to directly engage demons—that was left to their half-human offspring. If it weren't for the new demands of the treaty, Leksander would have been by Erelah's side constantly.

Lucian nodded his approval to their brother. "Leksander, you should go. See what you can find out. But this family of five doesn't sound like the mercenaries that Tytus managed to summon."

Leksander stepped up to Erelah's side, and Leonidas's heart almost broke with the yearning look on his brother's face—like he was begging for scraps of attention from this angeling he was desperately in love with.

"There has to be some connection," Leksander said, excitement working into his voice. No doubt because he would spend time with his gorgeous angeling. "I'll find out what I can and report back."

Lucian nodded again then tipped his head to Leonidas. "I think we have things under control here."

Erelah looked a little startled, like she had just now realized Leonidas was in the room. She threw him a pinched look. "Have you found your mate yet?" she asked bluntly. Angelings were odd—tact didn't seem programmed into their DNA.

"Working on it." He gave her a small salute.

Behind her back, Leksander was shrinking away. Leonidas was dying to know if the two had discussed it— the fact that Leksander needed a mate as well as Leonidas —but he sure as hell wasn't bringing it up.

Erelah seemed to have already wiped that incidental thought from her mind. She turned to Lucian. "With Markos's help, I'm sure we'll track down the source of the scourge."

She was back in full warrior angel mode as she whirled around and strode back out of the gaping open door. Leksander hurried after her, and Leonidas tried to not pity his brother... but it was difficult.

He and Lucian watched them go, and once they were out of earshot, Lucian said, "You know he's waiting for you, right?"

Leonidas cocked an eyebrow. "Waiting for me how?" Leksander had to fulfill the treaty just as much as Leonidas did—but as far as he could tell, Leksander hadn't made a move on that, despite his massive harassment of Leonidas to get busy with finding a mate.

Lucian frowned. "He's waiting for you to fail."

Leonidas leaned back and tried not to be offended. "Thanks for the confidence."

His brother shook his head. "It's not that. It's just that he..." Lucian hesitated to say it out loud, but it finally dawned on Leonidas what he was talking about.

Leonidas nodded slowly. "If I don't find a mate or go wyvern before I can spawn a dragonling, that means he doesn't have to give up on her. He can keep puppy-dogging after Erelah until his own wyvern shows up and puts an end to it. And him."

Lucian nodded.

"That's fucking insane." Leonidas's anger was rising up. If he had to buck up and do his duty here, then Leksander should have to do the same. "He'd really rather *die* than be with someone else?" Leonidas didn't understand this love thing. *Clearly.*

"Leksander will do his duty," Lucian growled in defense of their brother. "I've talked to him about it. He will make it happen if the treaty depends on it. But if it doesn't…"

Leonidas scowled. "You've already approved this." It was an accusation. But Lucian was King now, and his word carried weight. If the treaty was already screwed because Leonidas couldn't get his shit together, then Lucian would give Leksander a pass. Let him die with his unrequited love still intact. "That's the wrong choice, Lucian."

"It's not yours to make." Lucian shook his head. "But don't worry about any of that. Or the demons in Seattle. I've got all that covered. You have only one job."

Leonidas smirked, remembering he had a hot date waiting for him. "Knock up a witch. Got it."

Lucian huffed a small laugh and just shook his head.

"See you later, bro." Leonidas hustled out the door.

Chapter Four

ALL THE WAY DOWN THE MOUNTAIN INTO SEATTLE, Rosalyn wondered if she had lost her mind.

She was fucking with *dragons!*

Well, not literally fucking with dragons—at least, she hoped it wouldn't get that far. Not that she would necessarily mind… she gripped the steering wheel of her ancient Prius a little harder, then banged her fist on it. *No!* For the love of magic, she had to stop thinking of the shifter prince like he was just another hot guy. He was *a mark,* nothing else. Yes, he had some kind of weird magic thing where he needed to find a mate and make a baby. Great—good for him. He could carry on with that once she was done getting the small pound of flesh she needed to fix everything wrong with her life.

The only thing was, when she started out this whole crazy plan, she thought she was dealing with ordinary wolf shifters. Those she could handle, no problem. Dragon shifters, though… what did she know about them? Almost nothing. Except that the healing power of their blood was supposed to be a hundred times stronger than any spell, powder, or crystal… and vastly more powerful than normal shifter blood. Wolves and bears and freaking cheetahs, or whatever else was out there, were mostly human-like. Yeah, they shifted. Sure, they were strong and healed up fast. But they weren't immortal. Dragons lived a hella long time—even longer than witches who usually could conjure their way into the triple digits pretty reliably just with health and beauty spells. Not her mom, of course. She didn't conjure anything anymore. And Rosalyn wasn't exactly a practicing witch, either. But she could see the evidence in the covens she dealt with. Some of those crones were well past their 120th birthday and still looked like supermodels.

But… *dragons.* What was she getting herself into? Pissing off someone who breathed fire and had boulder-crushing talons seemed like a bad idea… and she was about to cross one in a major way.

She'd spent the whole drive going back and forth on this—either this would totally work even better than she thought or she was fucking crazy to even try. She'd just about settled on the clear truth that she was a certifiable nutjob for taking this on when she pulled into the back parking lot of her shop. It was on the outskirts of Seattle, bridging the area between the shifter gang territories and the domain of the downtown covens. Rosalyn could barely afford the rent, even with the lousy neighborhood, but anything closer to the more prosperous covens was ridiculously expensive. Those witches might not want her and her mother in their precious covens, but they were more than happy to slum down to her little shop for their potions and herbs and the occasional crystal or medieval-era talisman. She didn't know how to cast the spells herself, given what happened with her mom and their situation, but the hex that kept her mother from practicing didn't mean she forgot the ingredients for potions or where to get them. Rosalyn was as schooled in how to obtain mugwort and yarrow and deadly angel wing mushrooms as any practicing witch. Plus she'd recently scored some spell books from a couple traveling witches and a few less-than-reputable dealers in artifacts, so she'd been teaching herself some basic casting. But mostly, she'd always made sure she had high-quality goods—even the illegal variety—and her shop had earned a reputation for dealing in top-shelf, low-priced goods for the witching community.

A community that had no interest in letting her join.

Rosalyn parked her car and stepped out, teetering on her black heels. She straightened down her skirt, which had hiked up practically to her hips during the long drive. She never dressed up in this sort of thing, and the heels were borrowed from the back of her mother's closet, where all the real—i.e. not conjured—fancy clothes had been stashed when she was banished.

Rosalyn strode toward the back door of the shop. She and her mom slept in two small bedrooms at the back, right next to the storage room, their tiny bathroom, and an even smaller kitchenette. At least they had a shower and tub now, complete with hot running water. Rosalyn had bartered some questionable love potions and a month's worth of sex with a big, sweaty construction guy to build those. Prior to that, they'd been taking sponge baths with cold sink water and occasionally dropping by the homeless shelter for a real shower.

Being a down-and-out witch was pretty much a nightmare… and it had been that way most of Rosalyn's life. The part she could remember anyway. She had gauzy dreams of their life *before*—back when they were part of the coven and everything was magical and beautiful. And dammit, if she had to steal a little dragon blood to get that back, then *fine.* She'd take whatever fire-breathing risk came with it. Especially with her mom being sick now... Rosalyn was running out of time.

She gingerly stepped over the cracked pavement of the back parking lot with her high heels. The things were damn treacherous now that she was out of the pristine and upscale beauty of the dragons' keep. They must have some kind of cloaking spell to keep it from being discoverable by the rest of the magical world, given she'd never even heard rumors of a keep full of dragons tucked in the mountains outside Seattle. She still didn't know where it was precisely —they'd kept all the women answering the WildLove post blindfolded on the way in. Some hulking goon—probably another dragon, now that she thought about it—had met them at the prearranged parking spot, then piled them into a bus that drove them to the keep. The blindfolds were magic because all her efforts at peeking were thwarted. But she'd tracked the travel time, half convinced they were being kidnapped, not actually playing this Mating Game as advertised. But they did eventually land at the sumptuous keep, and it was like being transported to Oz. Rosalyn had no trouble believing the billionaire part of the WildLove post. And now that she knew they were dragons, it made sense—even the lowest covens could magic up a fortune during their long lives, and dragons lived even longer. Five hundred years, according to one Leonidas Smoke.

Rosalyn tried to open the back door of her shop, but it was locked. She let out a soft curse when she realized she only had the car key—she'd left the rest of her keychain at home, trying to travel light with minimal places to tuck things in her slinky black dress. She cursed again as she trudged around the back, past the abandoned shoe store next to her shop, down the grimy alleyway that stunk of Athenian food from the restaurant next door, and around to the front. It was a freaking obstacle course in her high heels, dodging grease spots and decaying vegetable matter. She was so busy watching her feet, making sure she didn't fall and crack her head for an ignominious death in a rancid Seattle alley that she didn't notice there was someone in front of her shop until his rugged brown boots nudged into her field of vision.

Her head snapped up.

The dragon prince. Only in jeans and a t-shirt instead of his GQ look from before.

"What the… how did you…" She was sputtering like a fool. She whipped her head around but didn't see his car anywhere. When she looked back to him, that sexy grin on his face was both heating her lady parts and making her flutter with nervousness. How did he beat her to her own shop?

"You did invite me to come visit, didn't you?" he asked with that deep-and-sexy voice of his.

Damn, he sounded delicious. Probably tasted even better. *Rosalyn!* Fuck. "Yes, but…" Her mind was spinning. She hadn't even had a chance to get inside and get ready. "How did you beat me here? Did you race your Lamborghini down the mountain?"

His smirk grew into a soft laugh, then he unfolded his arms and leaned forward. In a faux whisper, he said, "I'm a dragon, remember? I flew."

"You… flew." Of course, he did. She didn't know why this was blowing her mind, but it was. "Right." *Holy magic,* she was out of her depth with this. But there was nothing to do about that now—the man was here. She would just have to improvise. "Okay, then… um… won't you please come in?"

She stepped past him to open the door of her shop. Thankfully, her mother had left it unlocked, just in case they had customers, and Rosalyn wouldn't have to bang to get her to open up. The door rattled—the glass pane was loose in the chipped wooden frame, which let in a draft in the winter like a constant drip of bitterness.

Leonidas took the doorknob from her to hold the door open—for a brief moment, his thumb brushed her hand, *oh so softly.* She wouldn't have thought they had touched at all except for that spark passing between them. It seemed to race up her arm and then travel right to between her legs.

His eyes flashed, and she knew he felt it too, whatever the hell it was.

"After you," he said, gesturing her inside.

Rosalyn hurried past him and into her shop. She booked past the tables laden with clay and porcelain pots, past the collection of wooden staffs topped with not-so-magical crystals—scepters for the unwary—and scurried to the back of her shop.

"Make yourself at home," she called back over her shoulder as she kept moving. "I'm just going to let my mom know I'm back." She pushed aside the hanging curtain of beads that served as a door to the store room and glimpsed Leonidas checking out the wall of shelves that held her truly magical collection of powdered herbs and mushrooms amid tiny vials of pigs' blood and bunny tears, as well as her extensive collection of lesser crystals, the kind that could enhance spells. He seemed intensely curious if slightly amused—but Rosalyn couldn't waste time worrying about his initial impressions.

She needed to make tea. *Fast.*

"Mom!" she called out in a high enough voice to travel back out to Leonidas. "I'm back!" Her mom was probably resting. There were whole days when she didn't get out of bed anymore, the ravages of her cancer eating away at the last of her energy. But Rosalyn wasn't trying to catch her attention anyway.

She rummaged through a collection of tiny boxes—recycled Chinese food containers. They were perfect for holding tea leaves once they were cleaned out and dried—the boxes *and* the leaves. Rosalyn collected and grew her own. And right now, she needed something suitably strong to cover the acrid taste of the poison. Her heart was pounding like it was ready to jump out of her chest and do its own magic conjuring. Her hands were shaking with it, but she finally found the peppermint at the back. She snagged it, turned around, and practically bowled over her mother.

"Holy magic!" Rosalyn gasped, the jolt of surprise going through her entire body as she took a half step back. "Mom! Don't sneak up on me like that." She kept her voice low so Leonidas wouldn't hear.

"Sneak up? I'm doing good to move faster than a sloth on life support." Her mother scowled at her, instantly suspicious. "What's going on?" She was the spitting image of Rosalyn—that was obvious from the mirror—only her mother was even more beautiful. Same red hair, except her mother's had streaks of pure white-silver running through it. Rosalyn hadn't inherited her mother's beautiful green eyes. Instead, she got blue ones from her father, the asshole warlock that hexed her mother after he found out she had fallen in love with a shifter. Technically, her father was still a witch. Warlocks were true practitioners of evil, ostracized from their fellow witches and generally scorned by all. But Rosalyn always thought of him as a warlock in disguise. There were days when she wished she'd gotten the shifter's genes instead of her father's. Then there were other days she loathed the shifter who ruined her life so much, she was glad to have her father's blue eyes. If only they weren't a constant reminder to her mother of everything she'd lost.

Rosalyn shook those thoughts out of her head and edged carefully past her mother. She was frail now, and a stiff breeze could blow her over. "I've just got a customer out front, that's all." Rosalyn skittered over to a high, glass-enclosed cabinet with a rack of bottles on the top shelf, just barely within reach. The inaccessibility was left over from when Rosalyn was too small not to stay out of the poisons.

Her mother squinted as Rosalyn lifted the brass clasp that held the door. She carefully snatched up one tiny bottle of clear liquid—not really a poison, just a paralysis agent. Short-lived, so she'd have to work fast.

"You should go back to bed," Rosalyn said quietly, then took her tea and poison and hustled toward the kitchenette.

"I don't think so," her mother said, shuffling slowly after her.

Great. Rosalyn slapped the button for the small electric pot they used to heat water quickly for tea. She waited, tapping her finger nervously on the counter as the pot crackled and heated.

Her mother worked her way into the kitchenette, one cautious step at a time. "Are we poisoning the customers now?"

Rosalyn's shoulders dropped. Why did her mom have to be so curious about *everything?* Normally, it was cool, but right now... she could do without it. She eased past her mother in the cramped space of the kitchenette to the cabinet that held their three mugs—one for each of them and one for the occasional guest. Which pretty much never happened.

"I've got it under control," Rosalyn said as she brought the mugs back over to the pot. She filled tea strainers shaped like mini cauldrons—a joke gift she'd given her mother last year at Christmas. The peppermint wafted up strong from the leaves as she poured the hot water over them. Then she plopped a couple clear liquid drops from the tiny glass vial into one cup.

"We don't need to steal from the customers, Rosie." Her mother's voice was hushed, *thank magic.* "I hope you're not planning some kind of extortion scheme."

"No-o," Rosalyn said, drawing out the word as if that was ridiculous. It sounded unconvincing, even to her.

Her mother's face softened. "Rosie, honey, there's nothing you can do now. The cancer's too far gone. Let's just enjoy—"

"No!" It came out more harshly than Rosalyn intended. She immediately regretted it with the way her mother's shriveled shoulders hunched up.

Goddammit. This nasty business had her yelling at her sick mother. She softened her tone. "Mom, I promise I'm not doing anything stupid, okay?" She put the poison back up in the cupboard and closed the door. "Just stay back here, stay quiet, everything will be fine."

Her mother pulled herself to her full height. The imperial look she gave Rosalyn almost broke her heart—she could only imagine how beautiful and vibrant and powerful her mother had been before her magic had been taken from her. "I may not be a witch anymore, Ms. Rosalyn Thorne, but I'm no fool." With that, her mother turned on her heel and marched with an unsteady step directly toward the front.

Oh shit. "Mom!" Rosalyn hissed. "No!" But her mother wasn't stopping.

Rosalyn gritted her teeth. *Fine.* She would just have to do this with her mother watching. She scooped up the mugs and hastily followed, making sure she didn't spill the tea along the way. Her mother thrust aside the hanging beads and stepped out into the shop.

"Welcome to *Thornes and All* apothecary," her mother said loudly for Leonidas. "I wouldn't touch the red caps powder if I were you. Not unless you're planning on taking an extra special trip through memory lane."

Leonidas set the lid back on the ceramic pot of psychedelic mushrooms he had been inspecting, then he showered a panty-melting smile on her mother. "I saw the sign out front, but Rosalyn said you were artifacts dealers. I didn't realize you were a full-service shop." His eyes were sparkling.

"I'm Isadora Thorne, keeper of the shop. Is there something we can help you with?" Her mother's voice was the careful, professional one she used with customers, but Rosalyn could see she was already checking out Leonidas in her far-too-curious way. She *had* to realize Leonidas was a shifter—the broad shoulders, the muscular build, the gorgeous face. Either that or male models built like Olympic athletes were suddenly visiting their out-of-the-way magic shop.

Rosalyn bit her lip and edged past her mom, bringing the tea to Leonidas. Better to get this over with quickly.

"I made some tea." She offered the poisoned one to him. "Leonidas Smoke, this is my mother. Mom, meet Leonidas." She gave her mother a wide-eyed look of admonishment that was all for show. "My mother doesn't crash *all* my dates… just the ones with super sexy shifters."

Her mother eyes went wide, then she just blinked. Once. Twice.

Good. Hopefully, the surprise would keep her from asking too many questions before Leonidas drank his tea.

But the wide grin on Leonidas's face was almost unbearable. "Super sexy, huh?"

Rosalyn narrowed her eyes. "You own a mirror, right?"

His grin settled into a smirk. Then he gave a flirtatious look to her mother. "Well, it's easy to see where Rosalyn gets her ravishing beauty."

Rosalyn hoped the red tinge in her mother's face was actually the fever coming back, not a response to Leonidas's compliment. But none of this was important right now.

She needed Leonidas to drink his tea.

Rosalyn lifted her mug to clink against his, somewhat awkwardly, sloshing the dark brown liquid just a little. "We have a tradition at the shop of thorns," she said, slipping a quick look to her mother and demanding with her eyes, *Play along!* "A tradition of having peppermint tea for newcomers. A small sampling of our wares." Rosalyn gestured to the bedraggled but tidy shop. They might be breathlessly poor, but she took pride in keeping the shop neat and dust free. No small trick when you trafficked in magical powders. "We're not the most glamorous shop of magical artifacts, potions, and crystals, but we run a good business here. Reliable. Top quality. And as you can tell from our tea, we have the best there is to be had."

Leonidas raised an eyebrow and peered at the tea. Then he lifted the cup to his nose, and steam wafted across his face. "Smells nice." But he didn't take a drink, and the look in his eye was a little too sharp.

Rosalyn's heart skipped a beat, then did a jagged tap dance on her ribs. She forced a smile onto her face and took a sip from her own mug. "It's not too hot," she said with what was probably too overeager of a smile. "Give it a try."

His eyes narrowed a little, and it looked like a smile was trying to break out on his face, but he wouldn't let it. Then he held her gaze and slowly took a long sip from his mug.

Rosalyn restrained herself from doing a victory dance right there next to the barrel of gingerroot. The paralysis tincture would act fast and would work even in small doses. It should only take a sip or two. And a handful of seconds. He might take out the table on the way down—he was a big guy—but there was nothing too precious on it.

He smiled. "So, how long have you been in business?"

She smiled back, internally counting the seconds. "Pretty much my whole life." Somehow, it was easier to talk when she knew the dragon prince would be out cold soon. "My mom ran the shop when I was little, but I've been learning how to find all the best herbs and mushrooms and scout down the best artifacts and crystals since I was ten."

Leonidas held her gaze while she talked, taking more sips of tea as she prattled on.

She was so giddy with anticipation, her hand was starting to shake. She clutched her mug harder to keep it still.

"Business must be good," Leonidas said, "if you've been at it for so long."

While he drank more, her mother said, with a sharp edge to her voice, "Appearances can be deceiving."

Rosalyn shot her a sharp scowl. Then she quickly turned back to Leonidas and toasted again with her mug. "We do just fine, thanks."

Leonidas finished his sipping. His smirk was back. "I'm sure you do." Then his expression softened a little. "You probably think I'm some kind of spoiled rich guy who doesn't understand how hard it is to get by in the real world."

Rosalyn hadn't really gotten that far, but that much was obvious. She'd forgotten she was supposed to *want* to mate with this hot billionaire dragon. He probably thought she was a major-league gold-digger. Which raised her hackles, but *whatever.* He would be out soon, and their "relation-ship" would officially be over before it even began.

She shrugged. "Everybody has it hard in some way." But she was mostly trying to be nice. There was no way this cocky, sexy, super-rich dragon shifter had it hard in any way.

He seemed to take that at face value, giving her small nod and holding her gaze again as he drank down the tea.

She just blinked as she watched, and her heart thudded in her chest. The way he was tipping the cup... he was drinking *the whole freaking thing.* She swallowed. Far more than a minute had passed.

It wasn't working.

She looked on in horror as he tipped up the cup, finished the last of it, then handed the mug to her. "Deli-cious." The smirk was back.

Fuck. She took the mug from him and tried to contain her disappointment, but she suddenly felt unmoored, uncertain of what to do next. She looked up into those dazzling, sapphire-blue eyes. They were twinkling with amusement.

"Would you like some more?" she asked, her voice cracking a little in the middle.

He chuckled softly, and her heart sank. *Did he know?* How could he know? And why wasn't it working? These thoughts raced torrents through her mind, as he said, "No, thank you." He trailed his fingers around the rim of the urn of angel wings then turned that devastatingly sexy smile back on her. "However, I would like to take you on a real date, Rosalyn Thorne."

Shit. "I thought you were short on time?" Her voice still wavered with nerves. What was she going to do now? A real date meant... well, she didn't really know. It wasn't like she went on dates. But she was sure there was sex at the end, especially with the way he was checking her out again.

"I *am* short on time," Leonidas said and stepped a little closer.

Rosalyn's mother was keeping quiet, *thank magic.* But she had a look of concern that made Rosalyn's heart race even more.

Rosalyn put up a hand to keep Leonidas from coming any closer. "Well, now that you've seen my shop, we can discuss where things will go from here." She swallowed, set down the mugs, and took Leonidas by the arm, turning him toward the door. "How about if we discuss this outside?"

That wide smile was back. "Of course." He tipped his head to Rosalyn's mother. "Pleasure to meet you, Ms. Thorne."

Her mother nodded but kept her lips squeezed tight.

Rosalyn tugged on Leonidas's arm—carefully holding him by the t-shirt sleeve and not touching his bare skin. Skin-to-skin contact seemed to be the key to the magical sparking hotness thing that passed between them. She quickly let go as he followed her. Her mind was whirling, trying to come up with Plan B. Clearly, regular strength poison wasn't enough—she would have to double down and get some serious magic involved. Only problem being that she was no good at even unserious magic. But there had to be something in the spell books she'd acquired—she just needed a little time to plan.

She strode to the front and waited until they were both outside to speak. "Sorry about that, my mom's a little weird about me dating. I haven't told her about this whole..." She gestured vaguely to his ridiculously hot body. "...mating thing. Not until I've decided what I'm doing."

"Of course." Leonidas grinned, then he leaned in far

too close and ran a finger along her hairline, not touching her skin, but sending a shiver through her with his nearness anyway. "Your mother was delightful. Not quite as fiery-hot as her daughter, though."

"Yeah, well, times haven't always been great." She scowled, not wanting to spill all of her life secrets or that her mother was battling cancer right now. *Asshole.*

Leonidas frowned. "I meant that as a compliment," he said softly, moving even closer.

She forced herself to stay put and not back off. He was getting a little too close for comfort—and her body was responding way too much to that.

"I really do want to get to know you better," he said, and it twisted her heart a little with guilt because he sounded like he meant it. And she had just tried to—unsuccessfully—poison him.

"Maybe we need to get away somewhere, just the two of us," she said with an uncertain smile.

"I know some fabulous restaurants downtown—"

"No, nothing like that." She shook her head, her mind speeding up the lies as fast as she could. Maybe a little truth sprinkled in would help. "I don't run around in the same kind of universe you do, Leonidas Smoke. I'm not into fancy restaurants and lavishly decorated keeps in the mountains."

"What are you into?" His expression was open, and she had that knife edge of guilt again. He was taking this seriously. Of course—he was looking for a mate. And she was looking to steal something precious from him.

"Work, mostly," she said, and that certainly was the truth. "Taking care of my mom. Most of my life revolves around the shop. But my mom is here, always, so it's not exactly private. How about if you come mushroom hunting with me tomorrow? Just the two of us."

His frown grew little darker. "You're not afraid of being alone with me?"

She threw a little saucy attitude back at him. "Should I be?"

His expression softened in a way she hadn't seen before. "No. You'll never have anything to fear from me, Rosalyn. No matter what. I'll always do everything I can to protect you from anything that might try to harm you. Anything."

His words twisted her even more—as much as it sounded like he meant it, those were the words a man said to get a woman into bed. Or get whatever they wanted. In his case, a mate popping out a bunch of dragonlings. For him, this was all about *that*. Which was fine—clarifying, even—because this was just a business transaction for her, too.

She straightened her shoulders. "Right. So, a walk through the woods with the big bad dragon should be perfectly safe."

He chuckled a little. "Tomorrow?"

She nodded. "I'll text you the spot and meet you there —it's halfway to your keep anyway."

He dipped his head and looked like he was about to leave, but then stopped. He braced one hand against the battered and chipped door of her shop and leaned in close —almost close enough to kiss. "I'm very much looking forward to getting to know you better, Ms. Rosalyn Thorne." Then he kissed her on the cheek, and she couldn't help the small shiver that ran down her back.

His lips had barely brushed her skin, but it had sparked pleasure straight to her core.

Then he turned and walked his super sexy self away.

Chapter Five

LEONIDAS WAS EVEN MORE CONVINCED ROSALYN WAS *the one.*

It was the day after their encounter at her shop, and she was now marching ahead of him on a meandering path that wasn't much more than a deer trail through the trees. Her flame-red hair was bound into a single ponytail that bounced on her backpack, and she tromped through the woods in faded jeans and big, heavy boots. She was sexy as hell in that skinny black dress at the keep, but there was something about the worn seat of her pants riding against her tight bottom that was seriously turning him on. Or maybe it was the fresh-scrubbed look she had in the diffuse forest light, clean of makeup and revealing her true, stunning beauty. Or the flirtatious little looks she kept throwing at him as she led him deeper into the National Forest, a secluded part of the mountain range between Seattle and his House's shrouded keep.

"How far in do you normally go?" he asked. They had been hiking nearly twenty minutes, veering immediately away from the trailhead and heading off into the trees in search of whatever mushrooms or magical herbs she was hunting.

"Not much farther," she said with a small grin. Then she looked forward and kept tromping.

She was a mix of mysteries he'd spent the last twenty-four hours trying to decipher. First, she was a witch, and witches and shifters were natural enemies in the mortal world. Second, she answered the WildLove post—a witch ostensibly looking to mate with a shifter and stubbornly refusing to leave when Leksander tried to throw her out. *Then*, she tried to poison him. Leonidas smiled at the memory of it—the look on her face when he drank down her entire cup of peppermint tea was priceless. But strangely, almost perversely, the fact that she'd tried to poison him didn't dissuade him from believing she would make the perfect mate. There had been little danger. The poison wasn't meant to kill—it was a paralysis drug of some sort—and regardless, he'd easily sensed it and flicked some healing magic into the cup when she wasn't looking.

But *why* was she trying to poison him? And why drag him out here in the forest for some kind of mushroom-hunting date? She wanted *something* from him, badly... he just wasn't sure what.

If he couldn't figure her out, there was zero chance of seducing her into becoming his mate—if this dance they were doing was even about that. His brothers continued to insist that courting a witch was epic-level stupidity. He didn't tell them about the attempted poisoning, of course. That would just fan the flames. He'd spent his down time between "dates" researching every bit of information he could find about her—there had to be *something* in her background to explain the whole tea-poison-thing—but he had found little in the way of clues.

At least she was telling the truth about the apothecary

being in business for a long time. *Thornes and All* was well-regarded in the witching community, despite its drab exterior and sketchy location. Their business license showed Rosalyn must've been only nine or ten when they opened the shop, just like she said. What they did before that was shrouded in mystery—it was almost like they were off the radar—but two things stood in direct opposition that made this mystery of Rosalyn Thorne an irresistible intrigue for him. First, she and her mother were powerful witches. Second, they didn't belong to any known covens, and they ran a dingy apothecary in a rundown neighborhood.

Why?

He'd contacted the covens, under the ruse of being the alpha of a wolf shifter gang, but none of the head witches were willing to come clean. They professed to know little about the two witches running *Thornes and All,* some even questioning whether they were witches at all. But they most definitely were—Leonidas could taste the purebred magic on them both, and that one small kiss on Rosalyn's cheek told him all he needed to know about the strength of her power. He barely touched her, and it leaped across the gap between them. His magic was strong—his dragon magic alone was far superior in strength to her witchy powers—but he was also *fae,* thanks to a tragic love affair between his dragon ancestors and the Fae Queen of the Summer Court. Over his five hundred years, Leonidas had bedded plenty of humans and shifters, but that sparking magic only happened with the first and last witch he had ever seduced—*Meridi.* That had earned him a curse, and his brothers could easily be right that Rosalyn was magical fire he shouldn't be playing with.

But something wasn't adding up here, and the need to know her story sparked him to life almost as much as that magical sexual energy they tossed back and forth. The strength of her witch powers was intense, and yet… she didn't use magic as far as he could tell. If she had truly wanted to harm him, she could have tried to throw a hex or cast a spell—it wouldn't have worked because of the asymmetry of their powers, but she wouldn't have known that. Instead, she tried to poison him with a few drops added to his tea.

Why would a witch so strong abandon her powers?

There had to be some kind of darkness in Rosalyn's past that led to this state of things. Leonidas didn't know what it was, but he had tasted it on her from the moment they met. It spoke to some scandal, maybe. Something that drove her and her mother from their coven. Or maybe Rosalyn never had one to begin with. Maybe they moved in from a different part of the country, leaving home for some unknown reason and settling here in Seattle but finding no takers. Covens were notoriously closed affairs. Witches were powerful and ambitious and distrustful of outsiders.

Rosalyn had a secret… and Leonidas was determined to discover it.

If he'd learned anything about women, it was that you could please them in bed and lavish praise upon them all day long, but if you righted some wrong from their past—intentionally or not, as he'd bumbled into more than once—you would win them so hard to your side you could scarce pry them loose. In the past, the *prying loose* part concerned him, but now, every part of him itched to know Rosalyn's deep, dark secret… so he could be the man who finally gave her exactly what she needed.

Whatever that was.

In truth, it was his only hope of winning her. If she truly knew him—what he'd done to a young and beautiful and vibrant witch just like herself—she would do worse than poison his tea. Which reminded him—if she offered any magical mushrooms during their hike, he would do well to say no. His healing powers were impressive but not immune to everything, as his recent poisoning courtesy of Tytus showed. And while Leonidas's mother and father were both dragons, and his fae blood ran strong, there were many generations of human mothers in his past as well. His human side was vulnerable, and his wyvern was hovering closer, waiting to break free.

He should be careful.

"I'm starting to wonder if there are actual mushrooms in this forest," Leonidas called out. She'd tromped a little further ahead while he was lost in his thoughts, mesmerized by her swaying hips. "Or if you're simply luring me into some kind of trap."

Her head whipped around, the thick rope of her hair swinging full-circle. The flash of the fear in her eyes was quickly replaced by an uncertain smile. "How do you know I'm not dragging you out here to seduce you?"

He only wished. "I was planning on seducing *you*," he said with a smirk. "But ladies first, by all means."

She rolled her eyes and face forward again, speaking loudly but not looking back. "When I decide to seduce you, Leonidas Smoke," she said with a haughty air and a little more sway in her hips, "you'll know it."

He moaned a little, keeping it low so she wouldn't hear. The sassy ones always got to him more than the others. Which was why he handled them like dragon-killing angel blades—which was to say, he avoided them whenever possible. The eager ones were safer—not only did he enjoy a woman who was lusty in bed, but those kind never held out, baiting him, teasing him… trying to poison him.

Leonidas shook his head. He was well and truly fucked up if that turned him on.

Rosalyn disappeared behind a copse of trees, and Leonidas's heart rate kicked up a notch. There was something about her being out of sight that set his nerves on edge. Not that he feared she might spring some kind of magic trap—whatever she wanted to throw, he could handle if he was prepared—it was more a reflexive concern that he had lost her. Out in the middle of the forest. Where he knew other shifters and supernatural creatures liked to roam. Normally, a witch could take care of herself, but Rosalyn was a witch who didn't practice…

"Rosalyn!" he called out, picking up his pace and reaching forward with his fae senses. He tasted her—sweet lavender and wildberries and crackling blue magic—right before he sensed a scrambled mix of magical wards. *Wards?*

"Over here!" she called just as he rounded the copse of trees to find her standing at the mouth of a small cave.

He could see the faintest outlines of the wards scrawled on the interior of the rocky cave. The symbols had been drawn and then washed off—*hidden.* But not well, at least for his keen dragon vision and fae senses. The wards were incomplete—that's why they seemed scrambled—needing one final symbol to lock them into place.

He pointed toward the cave and narrowed his eyes. "What's this?"

She whipped a look back at the cave—quickly, as though she was afraid her hidden wards were showing through—and he took that moment to flick a small bit of magic toward the symbols. Their magic was weak, and he easily wiped it away. By the time she turned back, her wards had been disabled. They were for binding, but far too weak to hold the likes of him. And besides, they were incorrectly constructed, like a house of twigs that only needed a slight push to come crashing down. He could have easily brushed them aside, even if she'd managed to complete the symbols once he was inside the cave.

Inept magic from a powerful witch.

And another trap for him.

Why?

She hiked her backpack up higher on her shoulders. "This is just a little place I like to come." But her voice was pitched up. Nervous. "I thought it might be a nice for us to… hang out for a while."

He smirked. She was planning to lure him into the cave with promises of… sex? Making out? A kiss filled with that sparking magic?

It was a good lure, actually.

He played along, sauntering toward her. "I thought we were hunting mushrooms?"

"Oh, there are mushrooms inside, too." She backed into the cave, welcoming him with a sweep of her arm.

As he stepped inside, her eyes lit up. He had to restrain his smirk. If the wards had still been up, he would be completely within their reach—trapped if activated. And if he didn't have powerful dragon and fae magic on tap.

"There are mushrooms over there," she said, glancing toward the damp and musty back of the cave. Even in the shaded and somewhat gloomy light, Leonidas could see the ghostly white caps of some native fungi poking up between the detritus of the forest.

She obviously wanted him to wander back there while she scooted out and snapped closed her trap. But he wasn't ready for the ruse to be over just yet.

He stepped up to her. "Rosalyn," he said softly.

She was clutching the straps of her backpack with both hands. The pack was supposedly for mushroom collection, but it had bounced far too heavily all the way up here. He didn't know what was in it, but the wild-eyed nervousness as he got closer said it wasn't something she wanted him to see.

"Yeah?" Her voice wavered, and she was having a hard time looking at him.

He touched her hand—the one clutching her strap—and blue magic sparked between them. In the relative darkness, sheltered even from the dappled light of the forest, the crackling pleasure-filled energy was visible, dancing between his fingertips and the back of her hand as he trailed along it. He traced a long, slow line down her hand, then her arm, finally cupping her elbow. His half hard-on from watching her hips sway through the forest was now rock-hard and tightening his jeans. She was fighting the pleasure, but her eyes were half-mast, and in the quiet of the cave, he could hear her breathing pick up.

"I don't know what game we're playing," he whispered, ducking his head closer.

She was looking everywhere but him.

He released her elbow and drew a slow magic line up to her hand again then lifted his hand to cup her cheek. It was almost unbearably erotic, holding her like this, not kissing, barely touching, joined in magic and not breathing… "Do you even want this?" He meant the Mating Game, his touch, the kiss they weren't having—all of it.

Her lip trembled, then her electric-blue eyes finally met his. "Yes," she breathed. He heard two answers in that one word—her dark secret whispering with a voice of its own, *yes, I want to trap you in my cave,* as well as an invitation to bridge the gap between them.

Only the second part mattered.

He leaned in and brushed his lips against hers, not even really a kiss, just the promise of one. She quivered then held still as he pulled back, but not before she chased after his retreating lips. *She wanted him*—physically, at least, possibly as much as he wanted her—and that electric touch was still sparking pleasure between his hand and her cheek, making his cock ache and his mouth water. But he didn't want to claim that first kiss, not until he knew more.

"I need to know who you really are, Rosalyn." His words had the ring of truth and no small amount of begging—because they *were* true and needy. He hadn't felt his wyvern crowd his mind recently, not since he was poisoned by Tytus, but that was no guarantee of anything. He knew he was on borrowed time. And he was just as certain she was his salvation.

Her eyes were wide. "There's nothing to know." Her shaky breath stuttered the words—he could scent her arousal, the effect of his magical touch and near kiss—but then she stepped back, breaking contact.

He held in his sigh. "You're lying."

She jolted, and one eyelid gave a twitch. "What makes you say that?"

He had to stop himself from smiling—she was such a bad liar. Every body tell and reaction said she wanted him. Every emotion was writ large across her face. Fear, worry, lust—a grab bag that made her whole body quiver. He suddenly didn't care what her secret was… he just wanted to take her in his arms and kiss those quivers away. He could do it—of that, he had no doubt. The pleasures of his bed would take her mind away from whatever was worrying her.

Instead, he just gave her a soft look. "It's a lie that there's nothing to know about you." When this made her shoulders just bunch up more, he hastily added, "You're beautiful and smart, a sexy-as-hell woman with all kinds of smolder under the surface. There's *depth* to you, Rosalyn Thorne, and I really want the chance to plumb it." He let the innuendo lay heavy on his words, but he really meant it as more than just a come-on—although he was even more convinced that exploring that sizzling contact between them would be the first step with her.

And he needed to do it *soon.*

She gave him a saucy look and edged backward, toward the mouth of the cave, shaking her finger at him. "I told you before, dragon prince—no hopping in the sack until I get to know you a little better." She was easing her way out of the cave, and he knew she had every intention of closing the trap, even as she didn't realize it was no longer there.

He lifted his chin and stayed put. "What do you want to know?" he challenged. "What do I have to tell you to get you into my bed?"

She smirked. "Are dragons always this arrogant?"

"Only the good-looking ones," he dead-panned.

She stopped her backward progress and huffed a laugh. "Okay, Dragon Prince Who Is Extremely Good Looking—"

"Extremely, you say…" He took a slow step toward her.

Her eyes flashed—she held up a finger to stop him then started moving out of the cave again. "Go make yourself useful, Hot Stuff." She gestured with her chin to the back of the cave. "Get your hands dirty and gather up some of those mushrooms for me."

He stood still. "If I do, then I get to pick the location of our next date. And it's going to be in my lair."

"Your lair?" She almost choked on her laughter. "Is that what you call your hot bachelor pad?"

He softened his gaze but kept it locked with hers. His lair wasn't the ideal place, but she lived with her mother, and a hotel was far too impersonal. He would need to convince her she could belong in a place like the keep eventually anyway. And he was getting frustrated with all the traps she was throwing. What he needed was a good, long, uninterrupted stretch of time, trap-free and alone with her… and a chance to explore that electric touch in ways she wouldn't be able to resist. Then he could discover what was behind all of this for her.

He waited until the humor faded from her face. "I'm not interested in being a bachelor any longer," he said softly. "That's precisely the point. Precisely why I want you in my lair. Promise me, Rosalyn. Say you'll give this a chance—give *me* a chance—and I'll get my hands dirty in any way you wish."

He could see it flicker across her face—the uncertainty. Maybe a touch of remorse. Because she had to hear the sincerity in his words, his true need to make this budding romance work… but if she could just get him to stay in the cave and turn his back while she closed her magical trap…

"Deal," she said, and there was such softness in that one word, he had the overwhelming urge to ignore the game they were playing and simply take her in his arms again. Which twisted his stomach and gave him a whole different kind of panic.

"Deal?" he asked. "What are the terms, precisely?"

"You do my dirty work for me," she said, blinking a little too much, "and next time, I'll visit your lair. Then we can decide if we're…" She dropped her gaze to the bulge that had to still be prominent in his pants. Her eyes widened a little, she swallowed, then she dragged her gaze back up to his. "If we're sexually compatible." The way she bit her lip and clutched her backpack was just making him harder.

"Deal." He put as much sexual promise in that as possible, then he turned his back to let her do her real dirty deed—attempting to lock him inside her cave with broken magical wards. He strode to the back, swiped up a few mushrooms to seal his putative part of the deal, then hunted around for more, just to give her time to complete her task. After a short breath of time, he turned back to her, mushrooms in hand.

She was standing well outside the mouth of the cave, one knee down into the leaves, hastily unzipping the backpack, but with eyes glued to him. She froze when she saw him watching. He held her gaze and slowly walked toward the front of the cave...

...and marched straight out.

Her mouth dropped open, just for an instant, and her crushing look of disappointment made him wish he had kept the ruse for longer. She quickly dropped a mask over her expression, or tried to—she was like an open book to him. He could read every tiny flash of emotion, although he didn't know why. Maybe he was just paying extraordinary attention because she was literally the key to life or death for him. Maybe it was hundreds of years of watching women's faces, seducing them, tasting them— both literally and with his fae senses—keen for every small tell that would help him navigate the emotional minefield of centuries of trysts. All he knew was that her fast zipping-up of her backpack felt like a closing up of her heart—and that it had momentarily been open, revealing her true self, and he'd missed it.

She rose up from the forest floor just as he reached her.

"I just, um..." She was flustered, no doubt trying to figure out how her trap could have gone so badly wrong. Again. She slung the backpack over her shoulder.

He captured her free hand from its fussing with the strap and carefully placed the half dozen mushrooms in it. "Deal is a deal, Rosalyn."

She stared too long at the mushrooms, pursing her lips.

Was he crazy to try this? This woman wasn't within miles of loving him. He wasn't even sure she *liked* him. Two attempts to trap him definitely said *loathing* more than *lusting.* But the lust was there and real... and that was his ticket. Once she was moaning and screaming underneath him, then he could pry loose all her deep, dark secrets.

She finally dragged those beautiful blue eyes up to meet his. "Deal's a deal." Then she turned her back on him. He watched her hot little body stride away fast. He would use every skill he had, wrench every last ounce of pleasure out of her.

If he was lucky—extremely lucky—he might find the secret to her heart.

Chapter Six

Rosalyn was riding an elevator to the thirty-fifth floor.

On her way to see a witch.

It was the end of the day, and there was no one on the ride up. The elevator car was shiny and new with walls of polished steel that gleamed like mirrors. Her reflection showed a silvery version of her simple black skirt and white blouse—her attempt to blend into the office environment of a prestigious, downtown high-rise where one of the most powerful covens in Seattle kept their business. *Morgan Media and Art* was a social media and PR firm that dabbled in all kinds of online arts, enhanced by the dark art of their magic. They were a powerful force in the city, especially among the tech entrepreneurs who built billion-dollar businesses with their innovative products. Rosalyn never went to college—they never had that kind of money—but she studied the covens like a day trader hopped up on Red Bull, tracking their movements both in the real and magical worlds.

The elevator dinged, and she stepped out. Across the

short hall was the frosted glass wall of Morgan Media's front office. She'd only been here once before, spying, just to see how the other half lived—the beautiful witches who ran their empires, cloaked behind magic and the Internet. Most of their customers had no idea what they were, but some did, especially the shifters. Lots of them were still undercover despite winning more acceptance by the public every day. They had their own tech enterprises to run, and despite the general hatred between shifters and witches, they still did business with one another.

Business was business.

And that's what Rosalyn was here to conduct.

She sucked in a breath and willed her feet, which were wearing her mother's spiky black heels once again, to march forward. Just before she reached the frosted glass door, a trio of spectacularly beautiful women pushed through. Rosalyn nearly went down on the slippery, sparkling granite, but she managed to step back and not tumble as she gave them room to come out. They'd been laughing about something, but when they caught sight of her, the laughter and conversation died. They exchanged a round of looks that were curious, sharp, and baffled.

Rosalyn felt the judgment crawling up her neck like icy fingers. Did they recognize her? The tallest one was scrutinizing her. She had an exaggerated hourglass figure with a tight purple business suit that left her ample cleavage on display. Her lustrous black hair was like something out of a magazine, tumbling down her back and setting off her violet eyes. They were such an alarming color, they had to be magic.

"Are you lost, honey?" she asked, and her tone made it clear Rosalyn was a weed among flowers.

"No, I..." Her voice was weak and cracking, so she

cleared it and spoke more forcefully. "I'm just here to see a friend."

The witch's pencil-thin, dark eyebrows lifted, and her smirk drew up one corner of her mouth. "Is that right?" She gave a look to her friends—a blonde and a redhead like Rosalyn—and their wry smiles said they didn't believe Rosalyn's story at all. As if they just *knew* she belonged nowhere near the coven, even by acquaintance. She was the wrong kind of people for a place like this.

Someday, Rosalyn vowed, that would no longer be true. Maybe even someday *soon*.

She lifted her chin. "If you'll excuse me, I'm late." She brushed past them and slipped through the partially open door, trying to keep her head high and her stride confident.

The twittering of their laughter sent another shiver down her back, but she refused to look. The sound faded as the door slowly closed behind her.

The receptionist at the desk was busy examining her nails—she had to be a witch as well because her beauty was unnaturally vibrant. Skin glowing, eyes sparkling, a trim figure that was almost painfully thin under her fire-engine-red dress.

She didn't look up from fussing with her three-inch-long nails. "Can I help you?" It was clipped, as though she'd drawn the short straw with receptionist duty or something and couldn't be bothered to actually do the job.

"I'm here to see Alora Thorne." Rosalyn kept her voice strong, confident, but the woman still took several seconds to drag her attention away from her dagger-like nails and check out Rosalyn. When she did, it was a long, examining look from her teetering heels up to the bun of hair piled on her head. Another attempt to blend in, but these witches all had their hair down and casual and sexy. Rosalyn probably looked like an uptight librarian.

When the receptionist's gaze settled on Rosalyn's face, her eyes narrowed. "You look familiar."

Rosalyn's heart stuttered. She'd debated all the way down, all during the bus ride across downtown, whether she should spill that Alora was her aunt. No one from Morgan Media came down to the shop except Alora—she did all the coven's shopping, running errands for the other witches. Her aunt wasn't exactly a high-ranking witch, but she *was* a witch in good standing… unlike Rosalyn and her mom. Either that connection would get Rosalyn in the door, or it would out her as the daughter of a hexed witch and get her thrown out.

She didn't want to take the chance. "Oh, I just have one of those familiar faces. This is my first time at Morgan Media. Could you let Ms. Thorne know her appointment is here?"

The woman frowned, putting a single wrinkle in her unlined face. But she picked up the phone and dialed something. After a moment, she said into it, "You have a visitor."

She hung up and gave Rosalyn another deeply analyzing look. The woman could stare all she liked, Rosalyn didn't care, as long as her Aunt Alora came to the front.

Rosalyn pretended to examine the artwork on the walls —they seemed like real paintings, with brushstrokes and everything. She couldn't even fathom how much money Morgan Media made each year. Sure, she looked it up online when she was checking them out, but numbers that big just made no sense in her world. It was like the dragon prince's keep—money that big had to exist in some other realm, where all those numbers turned into things like sparkling granite on the floors and hand-painted art on the walls.

It didn't take long before the doorway to Morgan Media's main office slid open.

Rosalyn hurried over to her aunt, trying to get the jump on the situation before the surprise on Alora's face could work itself out into words. Rosalyn extended her hand as she scurried over, but her aunt stared at it like it was a live snake, so she quickly dropped it and just said, "Thanks for seeing me on such short notice, Ms. Thorne."

Aunt Alora blinked. Once. Twice. Then she threw a fearful look at the receptionist. Rosalyn kept a smile plastered on her face, but her heart was racing.

When Alora looked back to her, sharply, all she said was, "Of course." She hesitated a moment, then stepped back. "Please come back to my office." Then she gave Rosalyn a warning look, which she interpreted as *Keep your mouth shut.*

Rosalyn nodded once to show she understood, then followed behind her aunt as she pulled open the door to Morgan Media's inner sanctum and marched through.

It looked like any other office, she supposed. It wasn't like she'd ever been in one before, not that she remembered, anyway. It was funny, in a way, all these powerful witches stored in little boxes of half-height-walls that turned the big open space into a warren of cubbyholes. It reminded her of the Chinese takeout boxes she had lined up for her teas back at the shop. But mostly she focused on not falling—her heels were sinking into the plush carpet. Her aunt led her down one corridor, and then another, finally turning into a small office at the end. There wasn't much inside, just a rack of shelves holding mother-of-pearl and alabaster urns and a small wooden desk. Her aunt gestured her inside and closed the door behind her.

"What in the name of magic—"

Rosalyn's hands went up in defense. "Don't be mad, Aunt Alora."

She scowled, looking very much like her sister, in those few moments when Rosalyn's mother disapproved of something Rosalyn did or said. "Don't call me that here!" Aunt Alora hissed.

Rosalyn's shoulders sank. This was a bad idea. A really bad idea. But she had no choice.

"I need your help." She tried not to sound too desperate—but she would beg if she had to.

Her aunt glanced at the door, which was still shut. "We could have discussed this at the shop—"

"It can't wait!" Rosalyn stepped forward and beseeched with her eyes. "I have something. An opportunity. A way that I might be able to get us back into the covens."

Her aunt scowled. "That's not possible. You *know* that, Rosalyn."

"No, I *don't* know that!" Fear was twisting up her stomach. Her aunt hadn't even heard her out yet. "What I know is that a deal can be struck, no matter what, as long as you have the right bargaining chip. As long as you bring something to the table. Well, I can bring something to the table! I can bring something to this coven that no one else has."

Her aunt leaned back a little. "Okay. I have no idea what you're talking about. Clearly."

Rosalyn tried to calm the fervor in her voice. "I can get you *dragon blood.*"

Her aunt leaned forward again and scowled. "What did you say?"

Rosalyn nodded. "That's right—*dragon.* They're real, and I have access to one."

Her aunt's eyes went wide, and her hands fluttered a little bit. She turned away from Rosalyn and slowly paced back to behind her desk. She was thinking. This was good. Then she stopped and placed both hands on her desk, leaning forward and examining Rosalyn up and down as the receptionist had. "You and your mother have found a great niche in all of this. A silver lining. You've got the shop, you've got customers, you're building a good reputation again…"

Anger boiled up inside Rosalyn. "That's not enough!" Suddenly, breath was heaving in and out of her. She tried to rein it in, but she couldn't keep the venom out of her voice. "My mother—*your sister*—is dying."

Alora's eyes went wide, and she rocked back on her heels. "She's too young—"

Rosalyn lurched forward until she planted her own hands on the desk. "Not too young to get cancer. Not too young to die because she doesn't have any of the healing and beauty spells that are hers by birthright. *By birthright,* Alora." The anger made her hands shake against the wood of the desk. She didn't know how everything went down when her mom was hexed and thrown out of that other coven, the one uptown where her dad was still a high-powered witch, doubly so because he was a rare male among the fawning females. She was just a kid back then, but she knew that *years* passed before Alora ever dared to show her face at the shop. And her mom nearly threw her out—probably would've cursed her own sister, if she'd been able. So Rosalyn knew there was bad magic. "You *owe her,* Alora." She poured all the heat of her anger into the words. She didn't know if it was strictly true, but from her perspective, Alora had done nothing back then to help. Maybe she couldn't—who knew?—but *now* she could.

Alora's lips pinched in. "I've always done… I've always done whatever I could." But she sounded uncertain, and even Rosalyn knew that was bullshit.

"Yeah? Well, you can do *more* now. This is a chance for you to make things right. All we need..." Rosalyn drew in a breath because here it was—the pitch. "All I need is a little help. You help me get this dragon blood, and then the rest will take care of itself. You *know* everyone is going to want their hands on it. All you have to do is bring it to the Morgan sisters, and they'll say, *Everything's in the past!* and *Sure we can make a deal!* Because everyone makes a deal. *Everyone.* When there's something they want."

She could see her aunt's mind whirling, processing all this new information, but the core of it was pretty basic. The covens were constantly in a battle to one-up each other. To be the one with the prized hoard of dragon blood to juice their spells? They'd do just about anything for that. Including letting the daughter of a disgraced witch join their coven. It wasn't like Rosalyn's mom was banished from Morgan Media—her dad's coven was one of their uptown rivals. Which made it even better— Morgan could rub their noses in it. Even Morgan Media wouldn't let in her mother—that was just inviting a war between the covens—but that didn't matter. Once Rosalyn had the blood, she could heal her mother, join the coven, and then learn the health and beauty spells *herself.* Then no one could stop her from using them on her mom. Rosalyn could bring back her health and her beauty and her right to a long life.

But first, Rosalyn had to get back on the inside.

"So, you have this blood?" Alora asked, her eyes narrowing to slits. "How do we know it's dragon blood?"

"I don't have it yet," Rosalyn said, tightly. "But I'll get it. The problem is I haven't learned the spells, Alora. I need help to trap him."

Her face scrunched up. *"Trap him?* What makes you think you can trap a dragon?"

Rosalyn's fist bunched up, but she kept it on the surface of the desk. "I *know* I can trap him because he's already invited me to his lair!" She was spitting out the words. "He wants to have sex with me, okay? He trusts me. I've got him thinking I'm seriously interested in him. It's my opening, Alora, but I'm running out of time. He'll get suspicious, eventually. I need an immobilizing spell *now.*"

Alora was slowly shaking her head. "There's something not right about this."

Rosalyn's heart was back to hammering again. "What do you mean?"

"He's invited you to his lair?" her aunt asked, skeptically.

Rosalyn nodded. She didn't understand—why was that so unbelievable?

"Foolish girl," Alora said, coming back around to the front of her desk. "No shifter, even a powerful dragon, would invite a witch into his lair. It's some kind of trap."

Rosalyn shook her head. "He doesn't know I'm a witch."

Alora squinted at her, examining her face, looking for what, Rosalyn didn't know.

"I'm not lying about this," Rosalyn said, angrily. "What would be the point of that? You know what I want, Alora. I want a way back in! And this is my ticket. Are you going to help me, or not?"

Her aunt still looked uncertain, but she pulled in a breath, blew it out, and said, "All right. I'll make you a spell." She shook her head like Rosalyn was a pathetic idiot. "I should be able to bottle it, and it should keep long enough for you to use. But Rosalyn..." Her voice softened, and there was a hint of sadness in her eyes. "This is a dangerous business. You might not..." She hesitated, lips pinched again. "Your mother needs you."

"You think I don't *know* that?" Rosalyn's anger surged back again. "I'm doing this for *her*, Alora."

Her aunt nodded, chastened, then she turned and walked over to her rack of shelves. On the highest one was a jeweled box about ten inches long and three inches high. She opened it and pulled out a small twig tipped with a ruby jewel and a miniature silver blade. Rosalyn had seen a lot of artifacts in her time, but she'd seen nothing like this.

Alora brought the tiny spear back to her—it couldn't rightly be called a dagger, more like a surgeon's blade with just the tiniest bit of sharpness at the end.

"I'll conjure the spell," Alora said, "but you're going to need this as well."

Rosalyn took it from her. It looked ancient. "What is it?"

"A fragment of an angel blade." Alora's eyebrows were lifted, and Rosalyn wasn't sure if she was kidding or not.

"Angel blade? Angels aren't real."

Alora nodded once. "Neither are dragons."

She had a point. "But why do I need it?"

Her aunt went back to her shelf and rummaged through her pots, gathering up small pinches of powder and dropping them into her palm. "If you truly have a dragon who's invited you to his lair," she said as she worked, "and you truly want to draw his blood, you won't be able to do it with any ordinary knife."

Rosalyn gazed at the tip of the blade. Her stomach churned. The idea of slicing open Leonidas to steal some of his blood was suddenly leaving a sour taste in the back of her mouth. "But an angel blade can do it? Cut through dragon skin, I mean."

Alora finished gathering her supplies and returned. She handed Rosalyn a small vial. "According to legend, it's one of the few things that can." Alora waved her long-fingered hand over the pile of powders in her palm, and a small hurricane of blue sparks churned through and disrupted the tiny whitish pile. "This spell will immobilize him, but I have to warn you, once again, Rosalyn, that this is dangerous work. Even if all goes well and you immobilize your dragon, take his blood, and get out before the paralysis wears off—which is only a minute or two, let me remind you—then what? You have a legendary, powerful beast to whom you have promised sex and in instead you have snuck into his lair and stolen his blood? I can't begin to know what kind of wrath a dragon might wreak in repayment."

Her aunt's words sent a shudder through her. What would Leonidas do? He knew where she lived. She might have to seek the protection of the coven for her mother and herself. "I'll figure it out from there," she said.

Alora just shook her head and conjured the whitish powder into smoke and then slowly swirled it into the vial in Rosalyn's hand. Just as the last wisp sucked inside, her aunt flipped the small cork shut, enclosing the spell in the glass like a genie. Alora folded both hands around Rosalyn's and the vial, holding them tight.

"One minute," she said solemnly. "And have a plan to get out."

Rosalyn nodded and then swallowed down the dryness in her throat. "And when I come back, you'll advocate for me, right? If I have the blood, you'll get me back in." Everything hinged on that.

Alora frowned, and Rosalyn could tell her aunt thought she was a fool for doing this. But if Rosalyn came back with a bounty of dragon blood for barter, all doubt would be erased.

Rosalyn waited.

"I promise," Alora said.

Rosalyn didn't know how good a witch's word was, and she didn't know how to conjure the magical binding oaths she'd heard about in her mother's stories, but she didn't have much choice. She gave Alora a sharp nod, then turned on her tricky heels and headed out the door with her spell and her tiny angel blade.

Finally, she had *real* magic. And Leonidas would never see it coming.

Chapter Seven

The waiting was killing Leonidas.

He'd sent Cinaed, right-hand dragon to the king, to fetch Rosalyn from Seattle. No blindfolds this time, and plenty of chatter along the way, far from Leonidas and his brothers, who were still trying to harass him into finding a human woman for a mate. But the deeper he got into this with Rosalyn, the more he was drawn to her... and the more certain he was that she was key to pulling this whole mating business off. She *intrigued* him. That sharp tongue of hers amused him. And he was already craving another dose of that electric pleasure spark in her touch. It was a long drive from Seattle, and Cinaed might pry out of her the one thing Leonidas could not—why she was in this at all.

He paced the pristine living room of his lair as he waited, the minutes each piling on a new level of agitation. They weren't late, he was just *anticipating* having her here, in his arms, in his bed... it was trouble that he wanted that so badly. But he could practically feel the sensuous slip of her body moving against his—

A soft tone sounded from his front door.

He almost ran in his haste to get there, but when he opened it—

"Leksander!" he cried out, disappointed. "What the hell are you doing—"

His brother was a ball of agitation that rivaled Leonidas's. "I heard you're bringing her back to the keep."

"*Yes,*" he said, biting his tongue against cursing his brother. "She'll be here any moment. Please *leave.*"

Leksander just scowled. "Have you slept with her yet?"

"What the hell?" Leonidas growled, zero patience for more of his brothers' grumbling. "I told you I would handle this."

"Well, then, what are you waiting for?" Leksander's agitation was making his face turn red. "Get it over with. Or find someone else. But get it *done,* Leonidas."

His brother's fervor knocked Leonidas back a step. "Why the hurry?"

"I don't know," Leksander said sarcastically. "Maybe so you don't die in the meantime?"

"That's not it." Leonidas folded his arms and leaned against the doorway. "This has something to do with Erelah. Doesn't it?"

The way his brother's eyelid twitched and his fists automatically clenched, Leonidas knew he'd hit dead on—but he still didn't understand.

"I thought you wanted me to fail at this mating business," Leonidas said carefully. Somehow, focusing on his brother's tortured love life calmed his own worries. No matter how cursed he was, or how vexed by a certain hot, red-headed witch, he would never be tormented by love the way Leksander was. His brother was cursed in his own way—by actually falling in love, whereas Leonidas couldn't.

Leksander's teeth were grinding, at least by the way his jaw flexed as he chewed on whatever he was holding back. Finally, it came out. "I don't want you to fail. The treaty is too important."

Leonidas narrowed his eyes. "What if I do? What then? Are you going to finally tell her?"

His brother twitched, but stayed silent.

Leonidas's eyes went wide. "That's it. You're afraid to tell her."

"No." But his brother was far too vehement about that.

Maybe it was cruel, but Leonidas couldn't help poking at that raw and open wound. "Yes, you are. You're afraid that I'll fail, and you'll have no choice but to finally tell Erelah that you're hopelessly in love and want to bang her all night long. Only her angelic hotness might not be that into you. Because she's a *fucking angeling.*"

"Fuck you." Dragonfire was leaking from the corner of his brother's mouth again. He was a barely contained volcano, and Leonidas was a fool for provoking him. But Leksander needed to get the hell off his doorstep before Rosalyn arrived.

"No, *fuck you,* brother for interfering. I'm doing everything I can here to fulfill the treaty—I'm doing *my fucking duty.* How about you do yours?"

Leksander's rage released, suddenly, his fist plowing into the side of Leonidas's door, denting the solid brass dragon draped around his doorframe. His brother reared back and pounded it again, then once more. Then he pressed his fist to his forehead and stumbled back.

Leonidas watched coolly. "Feel better?"

"No." Leksander's voice was ragged, but some of the anger seemed bled from it. He glowered at Leonidas. "If I have to give up my love—my one true love *ever*—then you

can bed a woman you don't love. You've done it all your life."

"And *you*, my brother…" Leonidas glanced at his dented door frame. "…haven't done it in far too long."

Leksander shook his head, anger and dragonfire still venting, but Leonidas would bet half his treasure that his brother hadn't taken a woman to bed in decades. Maybe the full hundred years since he'd met Erelah. But he was sure the voluptuous angel was a regular feature in Leksander's beating-off fantasies.

Which was pathetic enough it finally wrenched sympathy from somewhere deep inside Leonidas. "My brother, go back to your lair. We'll talk later. I have a witch to seduce, a treaty to fulfill, and with any luck, a dragonling to spawn. Wait until that's done to worry about the rest."

Leksander pulled in a ragged breath and let it out slowly. "It's the waiting that's driving me mad." But his shoulders slumped, and Leonidas hated his look of defeat. Plus he more than understood—his own agitation, waiting for Rosalyn, wondering if this would even come close to working out, all of it left him horribly on edge.

And he shouldn't take that out on his brother.

He wanted to say something, but Leksander had already turned his back to leave—and Leonidas didn't want to keep him any longer, haunting his doorstep with his broken heart. He used magic to slide the door closed and slowly trod back to his living room, running his hands through his hair and trying to reset his mood. He needed to *not* be a simmering pot of anger when Rosalyn arrived.

Thank magic, he was somewhat calm when, only a minute later, the door chimed again.

He rushed to it, paused to collect himself, then slid the door open.

Cinaed was there, but Rosalyn had all his attention.

She had a fiery look in her eyes, her gorgeous hair was let down, and she was wearing a simple t-shirt and jeans that clung to her curves and made his mouth instantly water. She clutched a small, leather purse to her side in a white-knuckled clench that belied the smile that seemed plastered on her face.

Leonidas gave Cinaed a short nod. "Thank you for seeing the lovely Ms. Thorne here safely."

"No trouble at all." Cinaed tipped his head and beat a hasty retreat—Leonidas would talk to him later about whatever intel he had gleaned on the ride up. Assuming he could tear Cinaed away from his new bedmate, the human girl Rachel, handmaid to Arabella, their new Queen. Cinaed and Rachel hadn't yet announced their mating, but Leonidas wouldn't be surprised if it had already happened with the way they seemed locked away in his lair 24/7.

With any luck, Leonidas would be sealing his own mate soon.

"Please come in," he said with a sweep of his arm.

Without a word, Rosalyn shuffled past him into his lair. As he closed the door, she stopped at the edge of the entryway, staring at the vast white expanse of his living room—white couches, white carpets, white walls. To him, the bronze trim and copper vases and soaring two-story archways seemed tasteful and elegant. To her, by comparison to her ragged shop at the edge of Seattle, it had to appear an ostentatious display of wealth. Seducing her in his lair would require that he take her mind off her surroundings… which he planned on doing in short order.

"Can I get you anything?" he asked softly behind her.

She jumped, clutched her purse and slowly turned to face him.

"Something to drink or eat?" he offered.

She just stared at him. Then licked her lips. Working

up her courage? He wasn't sure. Finally, she said, "I've changed my mind about you." The uncertainty was gone, and the fire was back in her eyes.

"How's that?" His gaze fell to that purse she was clutching like some kind of shield between them.

She noticed his stare, twitched again, then hastily shrugged the purse off her shoulder and set it on the narrow entryway table that lined the wall. Then she stepped closer and peered up at him with those dazzling blue eyes.

"I want to know what it's like." She was suddenly breathless in a way that mesmerized him.

"What do you—"

But then she was on him, reaching up to pull his face down to hers, her lips mashing against his. Her hand clawed at his shoulder, trying to pull him closer, and what should have been a kiss felt more like a desperate attack. He half-smiled against her attempt to assault him with her passion and pulled back. Her eyes were wide and rimmed with fear. He held her cheek to reassure her this wasn't a rejection, then slid his fingers slowly across her skin, dragging the magic with his touch. His fingertips traced the curve of her chin then trailed slowly down her throat. He could feel her pulse racing. Her lips were parted, and her chest heaving.

Much better. "You want to know what it's like," he whispered, moving closer, "to be with a dragon?"

The hitch in her breath went straight to his cock.

"Then let me show you." He said the words softly against her lips just before he bridged the gap and kissed her. A proper kiss, not the grasping thing she had tried before—slow and seductive and sparking magic with every touch. He slid one hand into that gorgeous hair of hers, the other slipping to her back. He was barely touching her, no pressure, just his lips brushing magic against hers. Her breathing was erratic, and his cock was straining his jeans, but he was determined to make this slow and delicious. The tip of his tongue tasted her, and her mouth opened to him. He angled her head and tasted her deeper, but his own pulse was pounding in his ears now, and every part of him ached to touch her. He plunged further into her mouth, his hand fisting her hair. The small sparks where they touched were thrumming his heart and ramping up his need. His hand found the sweet curve of her bottom— he gripped her, pulling her softness against the hard press of his cock.

She gasped, and suddenly her hands came alive, clawing at his shoulders and digging into his hair. He growled, deep and low, surprised by his own intensity. He needed her *now*. Undressed. Hard up against the entryway wall. There was no way they were making it to the bedroom.

He lifted her from the floor and walked her back two steps, then pressed the length of his body against hers, relishing the moan that elicited from deep inside her. He broke the plundering of her mouth to trail hot, wet, sparking kisses down her jaw and to her neck. *Damn, she tasted good.* And that was on top of the magic that made him harder than he could remember being since… since Meridi… *fuck.* He shoved away that thought and pulled back from Rosalyn, determined to have her clothes in a pile by her naked feet in the next ten seconds.

Instead, she released him and put her hands out, stopping him. "Wait!" she cried, breathless. Her pupils were dilated. Her red hair was mussed and wild. Her t-shirt had ridden up, exposing her sweet belly. Nothing said *wait* about that.

"What?" he asked, hoarsely. Surely, she wasn't second-guessing this. He *felt* her body respond. He could smell her rampant arousal.

"I need… we need…" She was panting. "Protection."

What? He watched as she slipped under his arm to the other side of the entryway, back to her purse. *Oh, for fuck's sake…* the last thing he wanted was a condom coming between them. The full power of the sparking magic wouldn't be felt by either one of them that way.

"Rosalyn," he said, voice ragged. He turned to her, but she was hunched over her purse, back to him, radiating *leave me alone* body language. "Sweetheart, you don't need protection. You can't catch anything from me."

She was still fussing with the purse, rummaging around in it for her errant condom.

He edged closer, hands out. "I promise. Trust me, if it were that easy for a dragon to get a woman pregnant…" She was refusing to look at him, but she'd frozen, hovering over her purse. He tugged on her elbow to get her to turn. "Just let me explain—"

She whirled around and blew smoke in his face. He jerked back and blinked rapidly, but the room went wobbly around the edges. He stumbled backward.

What the fuck—

His hand found the wall of the entryway behind him. The smoke had dissipated, but his vision was still clouded, and he could just barely see she was clutching a small glass container. Whatever the smoke had been… *a spell.* Fuck! She'd cast a spell on him. His hands were cramping up, but he managed to wave one and conjure a bit of healing magic. His runes were reflexively crawling up his neck, racing to combat the spell he'd inhaled. Just as he was blinking his eyes clear, he saw the panic in hers. She whirled around and was digging in her purse again.

He took two fast steps across the entryway.

Just as he reached her, she turned, and he saw the flash of a dagger. She screamed as he grabbed her by the wrists and pinned her to the wall. The purse fell from the table and spewed its contents across the floor. A half dozen glass vials... *what the hell?*

He turned back to her. *"What is this?"* he demanded. He had to shake his head to clear the last of the spell.

Her eyes were wide with panic. "Oh, God, please don't kill me!"

Fuck. He wasn't going to kill her. *Obviously.* But what the hell was going on? He looked to the small blade in her hand—it was some kind of ancient twig with a ruby, but what caught his attention was the singing magic at the tip.

An angel blade.

Holy mother of magic. "Where did you get this?" he rasped out—the spell wasn't quite clear of his system yet.

"I'm sorry! I'm sorry!" She was crying, genuine tears of terror running down her face. "Please don't kill me!"

Leonidas softened his hold on her wrists. *Fuck,* he was probably hurting her. Her eyes squeezed shut, and her head turned away like she thought he was about to burn her to ash with dragonfire or some damn thing. She was sobbing, and a horrible mix of emotions was running around in his gut. Anger that he'd been played for a fool. Adrenaline from the fact that an angel blade was still humming in her hand. A rush of excitement that maybe, finally, he was seeing the truth about her... and a not-so-small stab of pain that had nothing to do with spells and tiny, deadly blades.

Because this was all a ruse. She hadn't wanted him. Not now, not ever. This was all about something else from the beginning. His wounded pride had no place in this, but it stubbornly stuck around, regardless.

Rosalyn was still crying.

He released one of her wrists so he could take the blade from her. He still held her one hand pinned to the wall by her head, but gently. "What were you going to do with this?" he asked wearily, holding it up. He waited until she blinked open her eyes, lashes wet with tears, fear still hunching up her body… but her terror at seeing the blade just made him throw it away, across the length of his lair. It landed somewhere in the carpet near the windows.

Maybe she wasn't interested in being his mate. Maybe she wasn't even interested in sex, although her body sure told a different story about that. *Fine.* But he wanted answers about this. All of it.

"I'm not so easy to kill," he said bitterly, then released her. He stayed close. She wasn't going anywhere until she answered his questions.

"No! I wasn't… I swear, I wasn't trying to kill you." Her eyes were still wide and terrified.

"Then *why,* Rosalyn?" He felt the weight of it dragging him down. Maybe his brothers were right. Witches were nothing but fucking trouble, and he should have sent her away, just like Leksander tried to do.

She was straightening up, back plastered against the wall to get distance from him, hands trembling. "Because… because…" He couldn't tell if she was too scared to get the words out or if she just didn't want to tell him. Her gaze flicked to the floor and the contents of her purse spilled on his entryway floor. He frowned and bent to scoop the glass vials back into the leather bag.

"I'm not going to hurt you," he said as he handed the purse back to her. "I just want to know. The tea. The cave. And now this… *why?*"

Her eyes grew more round as he spoke. "You knew."

He scowled. "Of course, I knew."

She just blinked and dropped her gaze to her purse,

still open with the glass vials inside—there was a half dozen, empty with tiny corks, but bigger than the one that held the spell. She slowly looked up with those tear-glassed eyes. "It was for my mom. She's dying. Cancer. I… I was trying…" Her lip trembled. "I only would have taken a little. I didn't want to hurt you."

Taken a little… "You were after my blood." It finally clicked in his head, and the pain was back, deep in his chest, making itself known. She hadn't wanted *him*—only his blood. And he couldn't even be angry… because if he could have brought back his father after Tytus poisoned him, Leonidas would have given anything. He almost did —gave every ounce of magic he had, trying to save his father and the others, but it hadn't been enough.

His head buzzed a little.

Rosalyn was still leaned up against the wall, shrinking back from him, shaking. *Holy magic,* he was hopeless at this. What made him think he ever had a chance at seducing her? He had no idea who she really was. *None.* But he had an inkling now. And she didn't deserve the fate he had lined up for her.

He held out his hand to her, palm up. "Give me one."

"What?" But her shaking calmed a little with the soft tone of his voice.

"One of the vials."

She pressed her lips together and dug one out. He dislodged the cork and handed it back. Then he shifted one of his fingers into a razor-sharp talon. Rosalyn sucked in a breath of surprise, but he didn't give her any time to be afraid—he quickly slashed his wrist and bright red blood welled up.

She gasped. "Oh my God. What…"

He shifted his finger back and tilted his wrist to the

vial. The blood slowly ebbed into it. He pumped his fist to make it run faster.

"What…" Her face had gone slack with surprise. "What are you *doing?*"

He flicked a look at her purse—yup, at least six vials in there. He nodded to them. "Those will take a while to fill. And it's more than you need." He drew his gaze up to her eyes. *Sweet magic,* she really was beautiful. And brave. Crazy brave. Trying to steal a dragon's blood to save her mother? And so young, too. The look of wonder on her face made her seem even younger, but she wasn't innocent—life had already done a number on her. Tossed her out of whatever coven she belonged in. Stolen her ability to magic some-how. Left her and her mom on their own to scrabble together a living. And now it was taking her mother, too? He saw how she and her mother looked at each other— they were all each other had.

"Don't give it to her all at once," he said, his throat suddenly thick. "Just one dose at a time, injected straight into the cancer site if you can."

Her lip trembled, and her eyes glassed.

He had to look away.

"*Why?*" she demanded. She almost sounded angry. "Why are you doing this?"

He didn't answer.

The vial was full. He took the cork back from her, capped the vial, and pulled another one out of the purse. He shifted a talon and cut himself again, deeper this time, to get the blood flowing faster. It worked. This one filled in no time. Blood dripped on the floor as he switched vials. She hastily handed him another one. Then another. He quickly filled all six that she brought and then flicked a finger for the one that held the spell. He filled that, too.

When he handed it back to her, he finally looked her in

the face again. Tears were dripping off her chin, but her brilliant blue eyes bored into his. "Leonidas—"

He ducked his head. "Because you needed it," he said hoarsely. He clamped his hand over the still-gushing wound and directed his runes and healing magic there. It sealed up almost instantly. "You wouldn't have been trying all this time so hard if you didn't need it," he added, wiping the leftover blood on his shirt. Red drops glistened on his floor. He looked up, and her eyes were still locked onto him. "Right?"

She nodded, jerkily, eyes still brimming with tears.

He had to clear his throat. "Not too much at once," he reminded her, softly. "If you need more, let me know."

She just stood there, looking at him.

"Cinaed will take you home."

She didn't move. Those blue eyes were shining, and the tear-tracks on her face were still fresh. He gave her a soft look. He couldn't be the one to turn away—she *had* to go first. She needed to turn her back and walk away with her prize. It was what she came for, and she got it. He didn't have the strength to throw her out.

"Rosalyn," he pleaded, but before he could get the rest out, she surged forward and threw her arms around him, hugging him.

It shocked him, and for a split second, he didn't react. Then his arms went around her, holding her. She was crying—sobbing, really, shoulders heaving as she buried her face in his chest. He held her head, gently, smoothing down her mussed hair. She quieted, and once again, he was helpless. He would stand here, holding her, as long as she needed.

Truth was, he didn't want to let go.

That pain inside—his wounded pride or whatever it was—eased a little the moment she was in his arms. He'd take that reprieve as long as he could get it, even if it was just a minute of standing together in his entryway. Then, just as his heart was calming and his arms were finding a settled spot on her back, she pulled away.

It felt like *ripping*. His heart, his soul… something.

She ducked her head, wiping away her tears with the back of her hand. She still clutched the purse, now full of his blood. The treasure she had been seeking. She wouldn't look at him, which made his chest cave in a little, just a little, just enough to let him know that it hurt. She edged over to the narrow entranceway table and set her purse on it.

He frowned. What was she doing?

She turned to face him, eyes bright, red hair tossed in waves around her shoulders. She held his gaze a moment, then reached down to the hem of her t-shirt and pulled it up over her head, dropping it on the floor.

His mouth fell open.

Before he could get words out, she reached around to unclasp her bra. That joined her shirt on the floor.

He lurched forward and stopped. "Rosalyn, *no.*" He swallowed. She was insanely beautiful—flawless skin, breasts standing at attention, nipples hard. Her beauty was stealing his breath. "You don't owe me this."

"No." A small smile tugged at her lips. "I *want* this." She started unbuttoning her jeans.

He crossed the span of the entryway, intending to stop her, but when he reached her, her hands grabbed hold of his shirt, bunching it and pulling him close. She tilted up her chin and peered into his eyes with a fierce look—it was filled with so much heat, it nearly stopped his heart.

"*Kiss me,*" she demanded.

So he did.

Chapter Eight

ROSALYN WAS LYING—SHE JUST WASN'T SURE WHO SHE WAS lying to.

Either she was lying to *herself* that she wasn't kissing the hell out of the dragon prince because she craved his electric-sparking touch more than anything she'd ever felt. Or she was lying to *him* that she wasn't jumping his body because she was grateful he gave her his life-saving blood. Both were somewhat false. Both were totally true.

But, *goddamn*, the boy could kiss.

His mouth was devouring hers, his tongue like electric pleasure in her mouth, making it ache almost as much as the spot between her legs screaming for attention. His hands were in her hair and on her cheeks and tilting her head as he nibbled and licked and *consumed* her with his lips. He had hardly touched her, but even the slight brushes of her neck and the hold on her cheeks and the tip of his tongue sparked that magic—it couldn't be anything else— was setting her entire body aflame.

Her hands flailed against the broadness of his chest, and she wanted to *feel him*, return that magical spark, pleasure him, but his kiss was leaving her senseless. Just as she got hold of his shirt and tried to tug it up, he broke the kiss.

"Rosalyn, are you sure?" he asked, and the breathiness of his voice said the dragon prince was as turned on as she was.

"So damn sure," she panted. "Take your shirt off."

His eyes hooded with lust, and she swore she felt that like an electric spark straight to her core, but then he lifted his shirt off in one swift motion, and her whole body reacted to the sight with an aching shudder. The man was so damn beautiful. She'd only seen those muscles rippling under his clothes before, but bared to her sight, he was like some kind of god of masculinity. Shoulders twice as broad as hers, muscles hard and carved and begging for her touch, and the tattoos—holy magic, *the tattoos*. A dragon and a stylized ring and a host of what had to be ancient runes. She recognized them from the book she had used to hex the cave. But these were inked across Leonidas's skin… *and they moved.*

He was standing there, letting her look. Making her wait.

She shut her gaping mouth and reached out to trace a single finger along the serpentine neck of his dragon tattoo. The magic sparked between them, gushing heat between her legs, but it seemed to affect him even more. A low moan rumbled under her touch, and her gaze was drawn to the bulge in his pants. Holy fuck, he was big. And hard. And nearly bursting out of his jeans. A thrill coursed through her that she could excite him that much.

"Be sure, Rosalyn," he whispered, his voice labored. "Be very sure. Because once I start, I'm not stopping."

She looked straight into his gorgeous blue eyes. "Take me."

He groaned, and like *that*, he had her pinned up against

the wall, all the fine artistry of his skin pressed against her bare chest. She gasped with the intensity of the full-body spark. His hands and mouth were on her, doubling down on that pleasure with nipping bites on her neck and squeezes of her breast.

"Oh, God, Leonidas," she gasped as his hot-as-sin mouth worked its way down her chest. His hands moved to the half-undone buttons of her jeans, and he practically ripped them off in his haste. Her pants and panties were down before she could blink. When she stepped out of them, Leonidas lifted her leg over his shoulder and slid that electric tongue of his right between her legs. "Oh, God!" she cried out, clutching his hair and reflexively pulling him deeper. He moaned as he lavished her most sensitive parts with his tongue and his lips and that magic that felt like it was electrocuting her with pleasure.

Her body trembled with the shockwaves, building fast and hard to an orgasm that felt out of control. Like it might consume her. She kept gasping and clutching his head and, when she could get a breath, crying out his name. She'd only had men go down on her twice before, and she had never understood why it was supposed to be so great, but those times were nothing like *this*. This was white-hot electric-heat pleasure that was making her twitch and moan and rocket toward an orgasm that was going to drown her.

Then he slipped his fingers inside her and pumped, and she literally screamed.

And came so hard she convulsed them both away from the wall. Wave after wave, she bucked like a madwoman into his face. Her shrieks would have been embarrassing if she had any control over them whatsoever. She literally rode that wave until it subsided, leaving her breathless.

Leonidas's fingers left her body, taking their magic with

them. He rose up and stepped back, and if they were done, Rosalyn could die a happy woman because *holy fuck* that was the best orgasm she'd ever had. Bar none.

But her heavenly dragon prince was undoing his jeans and liberating a cock so thick and long and beautiful it made her choke up. *Sweet mercy,* he was going to fuck her with that thing, and her mind literally blanked out at the thought. She just stared as he discarded his jeans, the full glory of his body and cock revealed to her.

So beautiful, she thought.

Then he was back on her, skin-on-sparking-skin, up against the wall. "No, you're the one who's beautiful," he whispered as he devoured her neck.

Had she really said that out loud? She would be embarrassed, again, if she could feel anything but the hazy afterglow of the most glorious sex she'd ever had. And that had only been what he could do with his lips and a finger or two.

There was more to come.

Leonidas's cock throbbed against her belly, the magic sparking there, and she could only imagine what it felt like *for him*—that sensitive tip against her flesh, those jolts of magic right where he would feel it most.

His hands were skimming her body as his mouth reclaimed hers. Then he reached to her bottom with both hands and lifted her from the floor, wrapping her legs around his waist and pressing his cock against the slickness of her core but not taking her. Not yet.

She shuddered with anticipation.

"I need you," he whispered hoarsely into her skin. "Hold on."

A whimper at the back of her throat was all she could manage in reply, but her hands managed to find a hold on his shoulders. He took her in one swift stroke like a masterpiece of fucking—hardly a jostle to her body but sliding in and filling her with a cock so large it literally cut off her breathing with the surprise and *fullness* of it. And the magic sparking all the way *inside* her… *holy fuck* had a whole new level of meaning.

"Oh my god, you're big." The words tumbled out of her mouth.

"And you're so fucking tight." Leonidas's voice was strained, and she realized he was holding still, waiting for her to adjust—to *breathe* again—like he knew it would be a shock to her. And that threatened to bring tears to her eyes because *fuck…* this man was already more sweet and considerate than any lover she'd ever had. First the vials of blood and now this…

"Are you okay?" he asked, peering at her. "Am I hurting you?" His concern was too much, too close, too intimate…

She wiped angrily at the tears with one hand then beat him on the shoulder with it. "No, but I'm going to hurt *you*, Leonidas Smoke, if you don't fucking *move.*" She blinked back the flood of emotion and stared him hard in the eyes. "You promised not to stop."

The growl that rumbled deep inside him was so devastatingly sexy and vibrated her body so intimately, that she nearly came again just from that. But then the soft-and-sweet hold he had on her disappeared, his grip on her bottom tightened almost painfully, and he pulled back and thrust into her so hard she yelped. She dug her fingers into his shoulders and tipped her head back against the wall.

"Yes," she whispered, and he did it again. With every thrust, she literally screamed or cried out until eventually, she was reduced to a mumbling string of curses and exclamations and whimperings of his name. He was taking her hard, grunting with each thrust, and the magic was a sweet torture ramping them both up—she could hear it in his breathing, more ragged with each punishing second, and she could feel it building and building in her core until it finally reached a pinnacle of quivering flesh sparking magic all around the steel hardness of his cock, plunging into her again and again.

Then she was pushed over the edge and convulsed against him, lifting them both from the wall. He kept thrusting, drawing it out, and she couldn't tell if she was screaming or crying, but it didn't matter because he let out a guttural groan that made her shudder with delight. He froze, buried deep, and she could *feel* the magic inside her reacting to the hot seed he was spilling as he came.

His groan faded, and his head dropped against her shoulder. He was panting, his breath hot on her skin, and everywhere he touched, always, there was that delicious, insanely erotic magical spark.

"Holy fuck," he breathed.

She couldn't agree more. Her body was buzzing so hard, it hardly felt real. Like she had floated off into another realm where sex and heat and sweaty magic were all that existed. Even when Leonidas pulled out from her body and set her on her feet, she didn't feel like she had returned to the real world. His strong arms and the wall were all that were keeping her upright—her legs were literally quivering as she stood naked, sandwiched between him and the wall.

She glanced at her clothes on the floor and cleared the haze out enough to wonder if she should take them and go. Carry the buzz out with her and let the world come back as she was leaving the keep. Maybe it would be easier that way. But the idea was moot—she was still working on standing upright. And the delicious soreness between her legs was already making itself known.

Leonidas's finger trailed along her jaw, lifting her chin and bringing her gaze back to his gorgeous eyes, now shining with the leftover buzz of his orgasm. She didn't know if it was as good for him as it was for her, but she had to imagine it was, based on the dazed pleasure on his face. "Don't be checking out your clothes," he said, a smile tugging at the corners of his mouth. "I'm not even close to done with you yet."

Not done? She just stared at him with wide eyes. She legit wasn't sure if she could handle anymore. "I don't know if I can…" She stopped and swallowed. Her voice was hoarse from all the screaming.

His hint of a smile grew into a smirk. "Oh, yes, you can." He leaned in and nibbled on her jawline, moving toward her neck, which seemed his favorite feasting spot. His fingers were twisting her nipple, just hard enough to blare a spike of pleasure through the orgasm-fog clouding her mind. He whispered against her skin, "It's not just my blood that has healing powers, sweet Rose." He drew a sparking wet line with his tongue along her neck, and the heat between her legs *throbbed.* God, how could he be exciting her again? "My tears. My saliva. My seed inside you. Every drop has magical healing powers."

Sweet mercy. "Are you saying…" Her mind was blanking again. Could this even be real? She tipped her head up to give him better access to her neck.

"I'm saying that if any part of you is sore, I just need to give it a kiss until it's better."

Holy fuck. "I think… I think I might actually die if you do that."

He chuckled, a deep and sonorous and sexy sound. He was nibbling his way down her chest. "No, but I want you to feel like you're in heaven."

Already there, dragon prince. But she couldn't say that out loud, even if she wanted to… which she didn't. She couldn't let him know how this was affecting her. *She* didn't want to know it. But regardless, she was robbed of the power of speech by his tongue running circles around her nipple, which was so tight it was almost painful. He tormented her for a while, and the pressure was building low in her belly. *Again.* How many orgasms could this insanely sexy man give her in one night?

An entire night? She realized just as he left her nipple and moved south that *of course* he meant to keep her. Not as a trap or a way to stop her from leaving with his blood… but simply because he wanted her in his bed. He'd told her that before. Multiple times. And unlike her, *he wasn't lying.* He wanted all that and more. So much more… more than she could give. But that thought was shoved away when his tongue found her throbbing nub and sparked the magic that made her whimper and shriek and orgasm like nothing she'd known.

"Holy fuck, what *is* that?" she gasped, even as she urged him on with her fingers digging into his hair.

"This?" He gave her another long, lascivious lick that made her yelp with pleasure.

"Oh my god!" she gasped. "Yes, *that.* Fuck! *Leonidas.*"

He chuckled again, and it was such a lovely sound— deep and sexy and full of happiness. She loved hearing it, even if he was laughing at her. But he stopped torturing her sex and rose up to face her.

"*That* is the reward of bedding a dragon, my love. But *fucking Leonidas* will have to wait at least a few minutes," he said with a wicked grin. "Dragons have legendary restorative powers, but even we need a minute or two before we're ready for more."

"A break is fine with me." She really didn't know if her

heart could take another one of those mind-blowing orgasms anytime soon.

He broke out into a full smile, then bent down to scoop her up from the floor. He carried her bridal style into his apartment, or lair, whatever he called it. For all that had happened, they hadn't even made it past the entryway.

"No breaks for you, I'm afraid." His smile was filled with sexy promise that said he wasn't sorry at all.

"What do you mean?" But her body was already reacting—held tight in his arms, the promise of pleasure sparking everywhere they touched.

"We'll start on the couch," he said, heading for some pristine white leather thing that seemed like exactly the wrong place to make wild, messy love. He smirked. "If we're lucky, we'll eventually make it to the bedroom."

Oh God.

He set her down on the edge of the couch but immediately spread her knees and knelt between them, lifting both of her legs up over his shoulders and forcing her to fall backward onto the white leather. He held her gaze as he licked his lips, slow and sensual... then he dived back between her legs, tongue first.

She shrieked again as the sparking hit her most sensitive spot.

Holy magic, what this man could do to her...

What had she gotten herself into?

Chapter Nine

The curve of Rosalyn's breast, as her chest rose and fell, mesmerized Leonidas.

She had been sleeping for a while, curled up, her delicious bottom snugged up against him. He'd managed to keep her in his lair, making love interspersed with naps, the whole night long. And while he should let her dream on, the tantalizing spark of her bottom against his cock had roused him out of a deep sleep almost ten minutes ago—he didn't think he could hold off waking her much longer.

But she was so damn beautiful when she slept.

Or when she was awake. And when she was coming with him buried deep inside her. There really were zero conditions under which she *wasn't* beautiful, but the sweet softness of her face at rest was enough to hold off his raging need to possess her again. At least a little while. Her dark lashes brushed her creamy-pale skin as her eyes moved under their lids. Sweet dreams, he hoped. Her rosy lips, swollen from their lovemaking, parted slightly and drew in a sharper breath. He was dying to know what dream caused that reaction, and if it was of *him* and their bodies intertwined as they had been all night. Either way, her movements were making his cock ache. When she sighed and arched her back, her nipples growing as stiff as he was, it was too much for him.

He slid a hand around the curve of her hip, going straight for the pleasure center between her legs. *So wet. Still.* He moaned, but the sound was lost amidst her sharp intake of breath. The spark of his touch right *there*, where it revved her the most, made her squirm against him.

"Good morning, love," he whispered in her ear. His voice was already hoarse with need. He slid down to angle just right to take her from behind. She gasped as the length of him eased into her. *So tight.* And the magic crackling all the way. It made him light-headed.

"Oh, God." She gripped the sheets and pushed back into him, meeting his slow thrusting with an eagerness that coiled something tight inside him. Need? *Maybe.* Desire to take their lovemaking up a notch in speed? *Definitely.* But it was more than that. He wanted to please her. To hear her moan because of *him.*

To do anything and everything to keep her in his bed… *forever.*

"Leonidas," she gasped. "Oh, God, I'm going to…" Then she just whimpered and drove harder against him. Something about that sound—every time she made that soft, desperate, thoroughly feminine sound of pleasure, it fucking drove him wild.

"Not yet, my love." He pulled out and rolled her on her belly, face down in the sheets—the pillows were long gone, tossed to the floor, and the blankets had been shoved aside as well. "But soon," he promised. With her flat on her front, he could edge her legs apart with his knee, just enough for his cock to slide past her bottom and take her deeply.

"*Oh fuck,*" she cried open-mouthed into the mattress. This position extended the range of his stroke, giving more contact for that magic sparking to ramp up the pleasure for them both. She squirmed under him again, gasping and moaning as he plunged into her. He held her hands flat against the bed, but her head lifted as she arched with the pleasure. The extra contact gave them both more sparking ache, but it was all about the slide of his cock into the delicious wetness of her body.

"Oh, God, yes!" she gasped. He picked up the pace to hear more of that—and she gave it to him. The cries and moans and fervent pleas of his name were making him crazy. He pounded harder, but he couldn't let loose the way he wanted—she may be a witch, but she was still mortal and fragile. She screamed and came undone underneath him, and as he raced toward his own climax, he dared hope that maybe, just maybe, this would keep her. This insane level of pleasure might convince her. *To love him. To mate with him. To carry his child.*

His heart was bursting with the need for it, and his head was dizzy with the idea of how mated lovemaking would be *even better.* Then the pleasure rushed over him and whited out any thoughts or feelings other than the complete and utter pleasure of having her. His groan was half roar, and he stilled as he emptied his seed into her. He couldn't help imagining what it would be like that first time —*mated sex*—even more intense and passionate and resulting in the blossoming of a new life inside this gorgeous body of hers. He was swept away in that moment, frozen, hovering over her, cock-deep inside, his heart swelling.

His mate. She could be *the one…* if only he could convince her.

He'd never wanted something so much in his life.

He came back to his senses enough to realize she probably was not comfortable. He pulled out, slid to the side and rolled her back to cuddle into him. Her sigh was full of contentedness. She reached back to wiggle her fingers into his hair, petting him in a way that, combined with the flush of post-sex afterglow, made him dangerously emotional. He slid her hand down so he could kiss it, then he trailed his magic-sparking touch down her arm and cupped her gorgeous breast. It was the perfect size—full and round but fitting perfectly in his splayed hand.

She let out a long breath. "Sweet mercy, is this a dragon thing?"

He grinned, although she couldn't see it with him behind her. "Being a fabulous lover?"

She eased away and turned to give him an incredulous look. "Having the endurance of a fucking Olympian."

He smirked. "If fucking were an Olympic sport, I would definitely try to qualify for finals."

She grinned but didn't laugh, just shook her head and rolled up to sitting, swinging her legs off the bed.

His heart lurched. Where was she going? "But yes," he said hastily, "it's a dragon thing." His words didn't slow her from getting out of bed. "Where are you going?" It was a reasonable question. Didn't sound at all panicked. He hoped.

"I think I left my clothes in the entranceway." Then she strode out of his bedroom.

What? He heaved his sex-sluggish body out of bed and went after her. "Are you hungry?" he asked. "I'm a mean cook, especially if all you want is eggs and toast. Because I'm pretty sure I have those."

She didn't even turn, just waved him off in her determined stride, naked, across his apartment toward the front door. He was right behind her, but she didn't say anything more, just scooped her jeans off the floor and had them half on before he could come up with something more to say.

She kept her head down, long red hair falling over and hiding her beautiful breasts. Her nipples were still at attention, peeking through the strands. His place was replete with the smell of sex so he couldn't tell if she was still aroused. He could fix that… but not with her pants on.

"You don't have to leave." This time, he was sure it sounded panicked.

"Yes, I do." She grabbed her bra from the floor and started working it on.

He was grasping at something to say. Something to keep her. "If you don't like eggs, I can—"

She stopped him cold with a look, then reached for her shirt and slipped it on. "I have to go, Leonidas."

His mouth was working, but nothing was coming out. He was standing, naked in front of her, and she was suddenly fully dressed and obviously ready to walk out his door. She stepped over to the entryway table, retrieved her purse—the one with vials of his dragon blood—and finally, turned to look him in the eye.

"I have to get back to my mother," she said, then pursed her lips tight.

Oh. "Of course." But that small gush of relief was followed by a hollow feeling in his stomach. "You remember my instructions about the blood, right?"

"Not to give it to her too fast. Not all at once." She bit her lip and held his gaze.

He nodded. "Then you're coming back." His heart skipped a beat. "Right?"

"No." She dropped her gaze and clutched the purse tighter.

The bottom fell out of his stomach. *No?* Just… no.

He moved toward her, closing the gap between them without thinking.

She leaned back but held her ground, staring at her feet.

He stopped. *"Rosalyn."* What could he say? He'd told glib lies to thousands of women over hundreds of years, and all of those words had inconveniently fled his mind. All he could think was, *Please stay. Please don't go.* And he would readily beg if he thought it might work. Instead, he touched her—just a fingertip trailing across her cheek and then her lips. They parted under his touch, and he could feel the heat of her breath on his skin. The magic crackled between them. "How can you say *no* to this?" He leaned in to follow the brush of his fingers with the touch of his lips, but she stepped back.

His heart literally hurt. Like a physical pain inside his chest.

"It's not you. It's me," she said, but he'd told that lie too many times not to recognize it.

It was definitely him.

Only he didn't understand why. "I thought—"

She took another step back. From that safe distance, she dared to look at him again. She was poised to run, between him and the front door. He could see it in her eyes.

"You're sweet and kind and… and you give the best orgasms on the planet." She gave him a pained smile. Leonidas had taken actual daggers to the chest. This was worse. "And *thank you* for the blood. Really. I can't…" Her eyes shone as she seemed to struggle for words. "I really can't thank you enough for that. But I have to go. And I can't come back."

"*Why not?*" He moved forward, involuntarily again, like he couldn't help being drawn toward her.

Her shoulders hunched up. "Please let me go."

The fear on her face gutted him. "I would never… I'm *not* holding you prisoner, Rosalyn."

"I know." She nodded, jerkily, like her nerves were strung too tight to make it smooth. "It's just…" She struggled for words again, then seemed to blink back tears.

"What is it?" he asked, lurching forward again, almost within reach.

She backed up and held up a hand. "Don't. I can't… just don't touch me, okay? That magic spark. That's not playing fair."

His heart was banging around in his chest. "You *leaving* isn't fair." How could he feel this way… *this much*… after so little time. But he knew why—he'd finally seen who she really was. And there was no way he *couldn't* be captivated by her.

Her face scrunched up. "I *can't* love you." It seemed like the words were wrenched out of her, but if they were hard on her, to him, they were like dragon talons ripping him apart. She gestured to him with one hand, the other clutching her purse to her chest. "And I know you *need* that. You told me. You need someone to love you and have your babies so you can live for another five hundred years and grow to be old dragons together. *I get it.* I just… I can't be that person."

His fists were clenched hard. He could feel his talons coming out, slicing through his palms, and it still didn't rival the pain in his chest. "You haven't told me why." His voice was strained.

"You're a *shifter,*" she said, low and tight.

He felt a cruel spring of hope. "Shifters and witches don't have to be enemies."

"They do for me." She was blinking back tears now, but they seemed angry. "You *knew* I was a witch! You've known from the beginning. Don't you wonder why I can't do spells or cast hexes or make wards that fucking *work?* Why the only thing my magic is apparently good for is making sex sparks with you?" Her teeth were clenched, and she shook. Like literally vibrated with her anger.

His eyes went wide. "I figured you had to leave your coven—"

"*Yes.*" She spat the word. "We *had* to leave. Forced out. And you know why? Because my mother *fucked a shifter.* Some hot-damn sexy shifter waltzed into our lives, took my mother to bed, and ruined my fucking life." Tears leaked from the corners of her eyes.

Leonidas stood mute, all words, all thoughts, banished from his head.

She shook an angry finger at him. "I am *not* making that mistake."

There was nothing he could say to that. He didn't even try.

She held the purse close to her chest, looking miserable. That, more than anything else, shook him out of the haze of pain. *She was hurting.* And there wasn't anything he could do about it, simply because of who—or rather what—he was.

She wiped angrily at her face with the back of her hand. "You're a good guy, Leonidas. A really good guy. This isn't your problem—it's mine. I know that. You deserve someone who can love you and give you little baby dragons and the whole fairy tale. You do." She was nodding now. "It's better this way. You'll find some other girl who can love you and give you what you need. You'll be happy. You'll be glad you let me go." Her eyes were too sharp now, too watchful. She edged slowly toward his door like she thought he might try to stop her.

Might try to keep her.

But obviously… he'd already lost her.

He never had any chance.

He just nodded—because forming words at that moment was more than he was capable of.

She dipped her head. "Thank you." She turned to go, then stopped at the doorway. "I really mean that. Thank you for this." Then she slipped outside his lair and down the corridor, out of sight.

She was a smart girl. She would find Cinaed or some other dragon to give her a ride home. He didn't have to worry about that. He didn't have to worry about her at all.

He leaned a hand against the wall and tried to breathe through the pain.

Leonidas waited until he'd collected himself.

He showered, shaved, dressed… and tried not to look in the mirror. He didn't want to see the pain in his own damn eyes. Rosalyn didn't want him. *Couldn't* love him. *Fine.* Besides, she was right. He would find someone else and seduce that woman into loving him. He would figure it out. Even if his first effort was a fucking sick joke. On him.

The second one had to be better.

When he'd kind of, remotely, in a theoretical sense, pulled his shit together, he went in search of his brothers. Leksander was out with Erelah, hunting demons in Seattle —*of course.* His phone went straight to voicemail. He was probably in dragon form or some damn thing.

Lucian picked up on the first ring, but Leonidas was already striding through the keep toward his lair.

"Rosalyn's out," Leonidas said, his voice circumscribed by a pain he hoped his brother wouldn't hear. "We need to bring back the other women."

"We… what?" Lucian cupped his hand over the phone, but Leonidas could still hear his mate, Arabella, asking what was wrong.

"Never mind, I'm coming to your lair." He slapped off the phone and picked up the pace. A moment later, he was pounding on Lucian's door.

It slid open to reveal his brother with an honestly freaked-out look on his face. Arabella and baby Larik stood just behind him, peering over his shoulder with concern. Larik was swathed in a magic-conjured blanket softer than anything human-made and looked as content and innocent in his sleep as Rosalyn had.

Leonidas wrenched his gaze away from them and back to his brother's concerned face. "You need to bring back the other women. One of them will have to do. I need to make this happen *now.*"

Lucian's frown was deep and furrowed. "I thought Rosalyn was here. At the keep."

"She's a purebred witch. She probably couldn't even fulfill the treaty. Besides, she left." Suddenly the anger animating him drained like a pipe bursting. "Just… just bring the other women back, Lucian. I'll make it work."

Even the alarm on his brother's face couldn't raise Leonidas out of the dark pit he was suddenly sinking into.

"Tell me when they're here." And with that, he turned his back on his brother and his mate and his dragonling. An adorable little family filled with a love he would never have.

That was his fate. He knew it. But he didn't have to look at it.

He would put on the mask he'd been wearing for centuries and do his fucking job. He would find a woman, seduce her, and make a dragonling.

If he went wyvern after that, it would probably be a blessing.

Chapter Ten

Guilt haunted Rosalyn all the way home.

She'd hurt him. The look on Leonidas's face… it was still twisting up her stomach.

The dragon shifter who gave her a ride—Cinaed—was sweet and sexy, just like Leonidas. Were all shifters devastatingly attractive and kind? She sure as hell didn't see that coming, at least not the kind-and-generous part. And if the rest were anything like Leonidas in bed, she could all too easily see how her mother had fallen for one. The sex was fucking mind-blowing. And it was more than that—there was a deep goodness in Leonidas. That she had a purse full of dragon blood in her hands was proof of that. She still couldn't believe that part. Couldn't believe she'd spent the night in his bed. It really was Olympic-level sex—something she'd probably never experience again. *But it was a trap…* she knew that, even if Leonidas didn't intend it to be.

This blood was her ticket back into the covens. And now that she was on the cusp of getting everything back —*her magic,* her birthright as a witch —she sure as hell wasn't going to mess that up by making the same mistake as her mother.

It was still early morning when Cinaed dropped her off. She stepped through the back door of her shop, the glass vials of blood clinking in her purse as she carried it inside. *She'd done it.* Her mother was still asleep, resting because the cancer was eating away at her body, but this was worth waking her up.

First, Rosalyn needed to wash off all the sex and get her head straight. Today was the day she would give her mom a cure! She rushed through showering, changing, hastily toweling dry her hair, then searched through the medicines her mother had tried—all the conventional ones and a range of supposedly magical cures—and found a syringe left over from a previous dose of something the doctors had recommended. Extra red blood cells or something to fight the worst effects of the chemo. She sterilized the needle as best she could then brought all of it into her mom's tiny bedroom near the back door.

Her mother must have heard her come in because she was already awake.

"You're back," she said, groggily, glancing at the murky morning light out the back window. Rosalyn had been gone all night, something she never did. Hopefully, that wouldn't come up.

"I have something for you." She settled on the edge of the bed and set down the syringe while she dug into her purse for a vial.

Her mother watched warily. Then her eyes grew round when Rosalyn held up the vial of thick, red liquid. She shot a look to Rosalyn. "What have you done?"

"This blood has powerful magic. It's going to *cure* you, Mom." Her throat was closing up as she was finally able to say those words.

Her mother looked horrified. "Where did you get it?"

Rosalyn was tempted to leave out the sordid details, but by the look on her mother's face, she was thinking something much worse than the truth. "I didn't kill anyone, Mom. *Jeez.*"

Her mother took the vial and tipped it up to the light. "The only blood I know that cures anything is shifter blood." She squinted at Rosalyn. "That shifter who was here yesterday. Leonidas Smoke."

Rosalyn nodded and bit her lip.

"He just *gave* it to you?" She seemed skeptical.

Rosalyn didn't want her to think it wasn't real… or paid for. She wanted no excuse for her not to use it. "I traded sex for it, okay?" Which wasn't true, but that was less shameful than what she'd really done. *Toyed with Leonidas's heart.* She hadn't meant to, not really. She hadn't meant for it to get that far. But that's what happened, regardless. And if there was anything she believed in, it was that you had to own up to the consequences of what you did, regardless of all your good intentions.

Or, in her case, less than honorable intentions.

She'd meant to steal his blood, not his heart.

If she could make up for that, once everything was settled, and she had her magic back again… she would. For now, she had to stay on track.

Her mother was still looking at her skeptically. "So this is really shifter blood?"

"For the love of magic… yes." Rosalyn sighed, took the vial from her mom, and started filling the syringe. "Not only that, it's dragon blood." She slid a sideways look at her mom—her eyebrows were hiked up, and she sat a little straighter. "I know, right? But it's true. They're real." Rosalyn hadn't seen Leonidas in his dragon form, but they didn't ask her to sign that non-disclosure for no reason

Her mom's mouth had fallen open, and she was staring hard at the now-filled syringe.

Rosalyn gripped her hand. "This is it, Mom. This is everything we need. Leonidas said to take it slow—small doses—but that it should totally work. And once we're done getting you healed…" Rosalyn lifted open the flap of her leather purse, revealing the vials inside. "I'm taking this to Morgan Media."

Her mother's sharp eyes snapped up to hers. *"What? You can't go there, Rosalyn."*

She gave a small smile. "Already have. Aunt Alora's going to get me in."

Her mother stiffened at the mention of her sister's name.

"This is my *chance,* Mom," Rosalyn hurried out. "I know you have bad magic between you. But that doesn't have to stop me from getting back inside the coven. Not anymore. Not with *this.*" She gestured to the still-open purse.

Her mother's expression softened. "The shop's not good enough for you."

Frustration welled up inside Rosalyn. "That's not it! I'll still be here. I'll still help you run the shop. It's just that…" How could she explain? Had it been so long since her mother had her powers that she forgot? That she didn't realize what it cost her own daughter?

Her mother was nodding. "You want to be a witch. A *complete* witch."

Rosalyn's hunched up shoulders relaxed. "Exactly." She let out a sigh of relief. "I just want to be what I was *meant* to be. That's all."

"What you lost because of me." The corners of her mother's eyes crinkled, and the green in them seemed to shine a little more.

Rosalyn hated that look, but it was true. And there was no point in denying it. She'd long ago forgiven her mother for the indiscretion that brought everything crashing down. "This isn't about blame, Mom. This is just about setting things right."

Her mom gave her a pained smile and stuck out her arm. "Then let's do it."

Real relief—the gushing kind—filled her now. She held the syringe away at a safe distance, so she didn't accidentally stab her mother, then reached out to give her a hug. They held each other for a long moment, and then Rosalyn let her go… before the tears could work their way loose.

Her hand shook a little as she tried to find a vein to inject. She'd had to do it a couple times before, for the other medicine, but this was way too important. She couldn't spill a drop of this precious gift-of-medicine, so she had to get it right the first time. Finally, the needle went in—and her mom didn't even flinch. Slowly, Rosalyn pushed the plunger, easing the dragon blood into her mom's vein.

Her mom's sharp intake of breath made Rosalyn look up. "You okay?"

"Yeah." A tentative smile was on her Mom's face. "It feels… warm. Almost like it's burning, but not really. Not bad."

Rosalyn nodded and focused back on the syringe, pushing tiny amounts, slowly, drip by drip into her mom. *Fiery dragon blood.* It made a kind of sense. She just hoped the magic of it lived up to the legends.

Her mom clenched her fist, the one on the side not getting injected with dragon blood.

"You sure you're okay?" Rosalyn asked without looking up. She was almost done with the first half vial.

"Yeah." But her mom's voice was a little breathless.

Rosalyn eased the needle out and held the spot, to make sure the wound closed and not a single drop of the dragon blood escaped. Only then did she look up at her mother's face. It was flushed like she had a fever, and her eyes had taken on a shine that wasn't tears—more like wonder.

"How do you feel?" Rosalyn asked, wide-eyed.

"Good." She fanned herself. "Hot. Can we open the window?"

There's was nothing but alley stench outside, but Rosalyn set down the syringe next to the vials and moved quickly to open the window. She frowned as she sat down with her mother again, then reached a hand to her mother's forehead. She was *hot*. Like running a serious fever hot.

"He didn't say anything about a fever." Rosalyn's heart banged around in her chest.

Her mother patted her hand but eased away. "It's fine. I'm fine." She leaned back on her bed and closed her eyes. The flush on her face grew stronger.

Rosalyn picked up her stuff, hesitated, then left her mother to rest. In the bathroom, she cleaned up the syringe and carefully stowed it away with the vials in a small cabinet above the sink. When she closed the mirrored door, she stared at her own reflection. Her eyes were bloodshot from lack of sleep, and dark circles haunted her eyes. She looked like hell.

How long would the blood take to work? Would her mother need more? There was no way to tell. And she couldn't exactly call up Leonidas to ask.

Suddenly, she was bone weary. Miraculously, the all-night-sex marathon hadn't made her sore in the lady parts, but damn, the rest of her felt like she'd run a hundred miles.

She dragged herself to her own room and nearly collapsed onto the bed. Just a little rest, and she would be back up to check on her mom. But as soon as she closed her eyes, she was falling down a deep, dark tunnel into unconsciousness.

Someone was shaking her.

Rosalyn groaned and buried her face in the pillow. *"Sleeping,"* she complained.

"Rosalyn, wake up!" It was her mother's voice, only different. Happy and way too zippy for Rosalyn's barely-awake brain to comprehend.

She dragged her face out of the pillow and squinted up at her mom. "What?"

"Wake *up!*" Her mom sat on the bed, bouncing her and swatting her bottom.

Bouncing? Since when did her mother have energy to…

Rosalyn came fully awake. She shook off the haze of sleep and scrambled up to sitting. Her mom's face wasn't feverish, and it didn't have that horrible sunken-in look the chemo had left behind as a parting gift. She positively *glowed.* Green eyes bright. Red hair lustrous.

"Mom?" Rosalyn was breathless.

"It worked!" Her mom smiled wide. Then she stood and did a pirouette to the door.

Rosalyn's mouth fell open.

"I haven't felt this good since… I can't even remember. Before the cancer. Before that, even." Her mother shook her head, smile wide. "That dragon blood is a damn miracle."

Rosalyn leaped out of bed, flew across the room, and hugged her mom hard. The emotion was just catching up to her, but she had no words yet. Just hugs. And a shaky laugh.

Her mom pulled back. "I'm going to make us some tea to celebrate!" Then she damn near skipped down the hall to the kitchenette. Rosalyn just watched her go with her mouth hanging open.

It worked. Which meant the blood was the real deal.

And she had her ticket back into the society of witches.

Chapter Eleven

"This is all you've got?" Leonidas asked, scanning the roomful of women.

"Leksander's working on it," Lucian said.

They were back in the throne room, the same setup as before, only "roomful of women" was a vast exaggeration. There were *three*. All lovely, but still—not much to choose from. Then again, that didn't matter. Any would do as long as they could fulfill the treaty. He reached out with his fae magic to get a sense of them. They were all ordinary humans, of course. No secret witches lying in wait, ready to spring a trap on him and steal his blood. One was a redhead but with green eyes, not blue. Still, he'd avoid her at all costs. No sense reminding himself what a fucking idiot he had been. Or what he would miss between the sheets.

Leonidas lifted his chin toward the ridiculously thin one keeping to herself. "The blonde. Send her in." He unfolded his arms and turned to stride into the interview room, closing the door behind him.

He ran his hands through his hair and pulled in a

breath. The blonde had a darkness buried in her past, something that had weakened her to the core. He could taste it—and that was probably his best avenue to exploit. Dive in fast, figure out what it was, then give the woman whatever would cure her inner torment. He could lavish riches beyond imagining upon her, but that wasn't what most wanted, not really. He would figure out what she needed and give it to her. Be her fucking Prince Charming, whatever flavor she wanted, as long as it worked. She needed to fall fast and hard for him. Besides, burying himself in another woman had always been the answer before; it would be the answer to Rosalyn as well.

Rosalyn. Fuck, he needed to banish that name from his thoughts.

The door opened behind him.

Lucian escorted in the blonde. "Leonidas, this is Ms. Emily Stratford."

Leonidas plastered on a smile—the kind he used when inviting a woman in a shifter bar to a quick bang in the dark. "Hello, Emily. Please come in."

Her smile was nervous, and her eyes wide. She skittered in, and Lucian closed the door. Her pale skin was flushed —she exuded a twitchy fear that chilled him—but under that was a mountain of arousal.

He extended a hand, and she took it, but she couldn't seem to look him in the eye. He frowned, but there was no sense in being coy. He kept her hand in his, caressed it, and pulled her closer. She gasped so loud, he thought maybe he was frightening her, but she offered no resistance whatsoever. And her arousal scent spiked hard.

His little dominant move was turning her on.

Okay, then.

He pulled her up hard against his chest, slipping a hand into her long, blonde hair and fisting it. He tilted her head, so she was forced to look at him. Her eyes were wide, but it wasn't fear—at least, not judging by the parted lips and heavy breathing.

He'd hardly spoken to her, and she was already panting. Which would be fine if they were in a bar in Seattle and there just to fuck, but this wasn't that. This was something altogether different. He just stared at her, looking her over, playing the dominant again, since that seemed to do it for her.

Her lip trembled. "I'll do whatever you want." She wasn't afraid. Her arousal scent was filling the room.

"Whatever I want?" He raised an eyebrow, but still kept it cool.

She nodded, jerkily, as much as his hold on her would allow.

His intuition was telling him to take her. Right now. Bend her over the chair and fuck her rough and hard. Allow her to come even as he made it clear she was there for his pleasure only. It was so obviously what she expected. And wanted.

Only the idea of it made him slightly ill.

He gritted his teeth. "Not yet," he said, coolly. "You have to do something for me first."

He swore to magic, she *whimpered.*

Dominance games weren't his thing. He pressed on anyway. "On your knees."

She dropped so fast, he was afraid she might have bruises. *Fuck.* Did he really have to pick the one dying to be a submissive? Then again, who else would sign up, *carte blanche,* to be the mate of a billionaire half-human who shifted into a beast? Someone clamoring for riches or maybe hot sex—that reputation definitely got around the shifter bars—or... someone who thought all the muscular masculinity of shifter males meant *dominant.*

His fist was still gripped her hair, but her head was bowed, awaiting his command.

Or for him to unzip his pants.

He should. If his cock was in Emily's mouth, that should be enough to shove Rosalyn out of his mind. He shuddered, but not in a good way. *Rosalyn.* Even conjuring her name made him want to move away from the girl kneeling at his feet.

"Look at me," he commanded.

The girl peered up at him through those long, blonde lashes, blinking too much and breathing too hard. She struggled to meet his direct stare.

"Tell me why you're here." He kept his voice cool.

She immediately dropped her gaze. "To do whatever you want. Sir."

Oh, for fuck's sake. "Tell me why you're *really* here." He kept a hard edge in his voice. "Do you want to mate with me?"

"Yes."

"Do you want to carry my child?" This game was getting quickly bitter in his mouth.

"Yes."

"Even if it risks your life?"

Emily quivered, but the hesitation was only a fraction of a second. "Yes."

She would do it. He could tell. He hadn't even fucked her yet, but once he did… once he dominated her in bed and unleashed the fantasy that she could lose all control and let him be responsible for all the wanton desires she wanted to express… then she would be welded to his side, obeying his every whim. He could have anything he wanted from her—total loyalty and devotion and dependence—in exchange for playing the Dom. It would be a hell of a lot of work, but that wasn't why he'd steered clear of submissives in the past.

It was because they were far too fast to bond.

Like the girl at his feet ready to pledge her life to him, if he would just take control.

Total devotion. Total love. *True Love.* He couldn't run fast enough from it before, but now…that was exactly what he needed. And he knew that as a Dominant, he could easily stay far from the danger of falling in love himself, whereas a submissive would trigger the treaty with her True Love in record time.

She was waiting for him to speak, just like a good sub.

His head was telling him she was perfect for what he needed… but his stomach was in full rebellion.

"Get up."

She hastily scrambled to her feet, head still bowed.

He used a single finger to lift her chin until she looked him in the eyes again. "I'm sorry," he said, softly. "I can't do this with you. I can't be what you need."

I can't love you. He cringed at the echo of Rosalyn's words coming out of his own damn mouth.

Emily took it about as well as he did. He could see her crumble inside. That dark thing that had happened in her past, that had emptied her out and made her crave this lifestyle, needing a firm hand the way she needed air… he was denying her that hope of conquering it. He felt a twinge of guilt, but there was no way he could make this work. He wasn't cut out to be a Dom. He liked his women feisty and smart-mouthed and sparking hot magic in bed…

"Please leave," he said to Emily.

Tears slipped from the corners of her eyes, but she ducked her head and beat a hasty retreat. She left the door open as she fled across the throne room, caving in on herself as she went.

Holy fuck, he was a monster, even when he wasn't trying.

He scrubbed his face with his hand. What in the name of magic was he doing? Turning away the gift of a submissive who would make this entire treaty thing happen without a hiccup. Was he fucking insane?

This was all about Rosalyn—she was haunting him. He couldn't have her, and it was fucking with his head. Meridi—the witch who had cursed him—was well and truly getting her vengeance. And in all honesty, he deserved it. He was horrible to that sweet, innocent witch in that long-ago time, and now he was truly fucked.

But the treaty still had to be fulfilled. He had to get Rosalyn out of his head before he could screw it back on straight. But it wasn't just his battered ego that refused to let her go. That story of hers was nagging at him. There had to be more to it. Her mom being seduced by a shifter—that was certainly possible—but there was something missing. And the mystery of Rosalyn was what had snared him in the first place. His mind was trapped in an endless loop… not trying to figure out why she left, but why she'd *stayed.* Why make love to him all night long only to hustle out the door at dawn? Why not make off with her booty? Something didn't add up there, but he couldn't just call her up and… *Cinaed.*

It struck him like a divine light parting the clouds—Cinaed had picked her up and taken her home. He had been instructed to pump any information out of her that he could. Maybe, just maybe, in the aftermath, on the way home, after escaping Leonidas's lair with his blood in a handful of vials… maybe she had spilled the truth to the talkative, easy-going right-hand dragon to the king. Women talked to Cinaed. Leonidas had seen him in action in the bars, long before Cinaed hooked up with his own possible-future-mate, Rachel. That's why Leonidas sent him to get Rosalyn in the first place.

He lurched out of the room and headed for the back door. "I'll be back," he said in passing to Lucian's questioning look, but Leonidas didn't even slow down. He took no time to cross the keep, and less than a minute later, he was banging on Cinaed's door.

He kept banging until the door finally slid open.

Cinaed was half dressed with an impressive boner tenting out his sleep pants. "Yes, my liege? Is everything all right?" He was glancing behind Leonidas to the hall like he expected a horde of demon mercenaries to be rampaging behind him. It wasn't like that hadn't happened recently enough.

Leonidas grimaced. "Sorry, man, I need to… talk."

Rachel, Cinaed's human lover and possible mate, showed up behind him, clutching a sheet across her obviously naked body. "What's happening?" she asked, a steely terror in her voice.

"Nothing," he said to her over Cinaed's shoulder. "Everything's fine. Just need to borrow your mate for a minute." Leonidas grabbed Cinaed by his bare shoulder and hauled him out into the hall, then used magic to close the door in Rachel's face.

"Sorry to interrupt," he said to Cinaed.

He waved it away, and Leonidas could see why Lucian trusted the young dragon as much, maybe more, than his own brothers. "What's wrong, my liege?"

"You drove Rosalyn home, right?"

"Yes." Cinaed frowned. "I thought she was… well, not in contention any longer."

"She's not." Man, there was a lot of bitterness in his voice. "But I can't get her out of my head."

Cinaed's eyes went wide. *"My liege. The curse——"*

"I'm *not* in love with her," he growled, but the surge of anger those words wrenched out of him felt wild and slightly unhinged. Too strong for what he should be feeling. Like it wasn't entirely in his control. He reeled it back in, spooked. He couldn't fucking afford to go wyvern, not now. He gritted his teeth. "She's just annoying the crap out of me, okay?"

This didn't seem to reassure Cinaed—if anything, he seemed even more concerned. He glanced at the door to his lair. "My liege." He swallowed and looked back to Leonidas. "I fear for you, sire."

"Look, I'm not wyvern yet. *Obviously.* Don't worry about that." But he couldn't help the tight knot in his stomach. Because he knew this obsession with Rosalyn was *not* a good thing. "What I need is to know what she told you on the way back. Or the way in. She's like this fucking puzzle I can't figure out. I just need to know what she's after. Why she came here in the first place. Not just the blood—there's something more. Once I know what it is, then I can let it go, get her out of my head, and move on to finding a mate and fulfilling the damn treaty."

Cinaed's brow was still furrowed, but he slowly nodded. "Are you sure? I mean, are you sure this is something you want to know, my liege?"

Leonidas's heart lurched. She *did* tell him something. "Just spill it, Cinaed."

He hesitated, but then said, "She was amazed that you willingly gave her your blood. She said it would fix everything for her."

"*What* everything?" Leonidas was ready to punch something. Possibly Cinaed if he didn't hurry up with this.

"Her mother." Cinaed nodded. "She said she told you she was sick. But there was more to it. Something about becoming a proper witch again. How this might win her way back into the covens."

Of course. "She was banished." Leonidas was nodding, but mostly to himself now. "But dragon blood is rare. She could buy her way in."

Cinaed shrugged. "Seems as though she could have asked for that favor directly. You have the power, my liege. I didn't say that, though."

"No. That's good." A hope quivered inside him. Cinaed was right—the covens would heed the wishes of the House of Smoke if put upon them. Back in the day, when demons were still plentiful on the earth, the House of Smoke wasn't so removed from the mortal realm. The covens had a tacit agreement to monitor for demons and vampires and other scourges, in exchange for occasional protection from the humans the witches hid amongst. The House of Smoke, if it insisted that a certain red-haired witch be considered for admittance, would carry some sway.

He could get Rosalyn into whatever coven she wanted. And that was the missing key, the darkness inside her that needed healing. She was a powerful witch who couldn't do magic.

And he could fix that—only she had no idea that was possible.

He shouldn't want to do this as much as he did. He should walk away. But if there was a chance he could heal the thing that stopped her from being able to love him...

"Thank you, Cinaed," he said with real warmth. "You may have just solved all my problems."

His frown was back. "My liege, you're not thinking of—"

But he was cut off by the pounding of boots coming down the hall. They both turned to look. Lucian was jogging toward them, a phone to his ear. "No, I've found him," he said into the phone, then swiped it off. "We have a problem," he said to Leonidas, coming to a stop next to the two of them. "Leksander found one of the women from before. She's dead."

"What?" Leonidas leaned back. "What happened?"

Lucian grimaced. "Drained by a vampire."

"Drained? As in all the way to death?" Leonidas scowled. The vampires weren't supposed to feed on humans at all, but when they did, they always left them alive. Bodies meant blowback, in both the human and immortal worlds. "What are vampires doing back in the city, anyway?"

"I don't know, but that's not all." Lucian exchanged a quick look with Cinaed, who was also suddenly on high alert. "One of the other women who answered the ad… Leksander says she was demon-infected. He cured her but—"

"Demons?" Leonidas exclaimed. "What the hell?"

"I know." Lucian shook his head. "I don't know what's happening, but the women, Leonidas…"

"They're being targeted," Cinaed said, his voice a low, rumbling growl.

Holy fuck. "What have I done?" Leonidas whispered.

"You haven't done anything," Lucian answered, forcefully. "But we need to bring them in. All of them."

Leonidas was nodding. "Of course. Bring them all to the keep for safekeeping until we figure out…" He stalled out. It struck him like a zap of electricity. "Rosalyn is in danger," he whispered, the words horrifying him even as he spoke. *And it was his fault.*

He scrambled to haul out his phone and dial her number.

"I'm sure she's fine," Lucian was saying.

Leonidas could only hear a buzzing in his ears.

The phone went straight to voicemail. Either she wasn't taking his calls or…

"I'm going after her." He turned and hauled ass down the corridor.

"Leonidas, wait!"

But he had no time for whatever his brother's concerns were.

Rosalyn was in danger. Demons or vampires or *something* was going after the women… and she was a witch without her powers. He shifted to dragon form to run faster through the keep and reach the central meeting room where the ceiling opened a door to the outside. He leaped up into the air and beat his wings so hard they ached.

What if he was too late?

His heart pounded as he pumped his wings faster, then he marshaled every bit of fae magic he had to boost his speed. The shock of the sound wave broke across the mountains as he broached the speed-of-sound barrier.

He'd been too late to save Meridi. Minutes too late to save a witch who loved him from small-minded people with their own reasons for killing. He couldn't save her back then, but he sure as hell could stop some unholy immortal force from snuffing out Rosalyn's beautiful and vibrant life today, just as she was getting it back.

The whisperings of a wildness nibbled at the edges of his mind, but he pushed it away—his damn wyvern would have to wait.

He had a witch to save.

Chapter Twelve

"CAN YOU AT LEAST TELL ME WHEN SHE'LL BE BACK?"

Rosalyn couldn't believe it—somehow her Aunt Alora was out of the office. Sure, Rosalyn should have called ahead. Which she would have done, if she actually had Alora's number.

"I'm sorry, she's out on an errand. *For Hecca.*" The receptionist was a different one than before, but her red-lipsticked smirk gave Rosalyn the chills. She knew her aunt was a pretty low-ranking witch, and Hecca was one of the two Morgan sisters who ran Morgan Media—Rosalyn hoped the errand wasn't something demeaning or awful. The Morgan sisters came from a long line of Morgans that had ruled their coven for millennia. The company was just the latest enterprise in their long and storied history. All that power for all that time… some witches could be down-right crazy pants, tormenting people for no reason. And *get the fuck out* if they actually had a *reason.*

Her mother's banishment was Exhibit A of that.

Rosalyn clutched her purse of dragon blood a little tighter and stepped back from where she hovered over the receptionist's desk. The woman went back to inspecting her perfect nails.

Rosalyn should wait. She should bide her time until Alora returned, and her aunt could speak for her. Then again, if Alora was coming back from some humiliation, a joke at the hands of the ranking witches…

"Is Hecca available?" Rosalyn burst out before she could come to her senses.

The receptionist looked up sharply and arched a pencil-thin eyebrow. "Available for *what?*" It was clear she didn't think Rosalyn was worth Hecca's time.

But she didn't know Rosalyn had a purse full of dragon blood.

She stepped back to the desk and set her purse on it. "Do you know who I am?" she asked the receptionist.

She was beautiful, using beauty and health spells like all the witches at Morgan Media, but the way she slitted her eyes made her look downright evil.

Rosalyn just met her judgmental stare with the calm, cool one she'd used hundreds of times in negotiations in her shop.

"You're that *hedgewitch,*" the receptionist finally said, a sneer in her voice.

Rosalyn couldn't help it—she flinched. No one had ever called her that to her face. She saw it used as a slur in some of the online forums where she lurked, the ones her mom pointed her to, saying sometimes the witches would discuss spells there. A hedgewitch was like a magical cripple. A witch who was so inept or broken that she couldn't use magic… so she relied on herbs and potions and crystals that did mostly nothing. Hedgewitches lived on the edge of society, just as Rosalyn and her mother did, working their shop, doing exactly those things. Isadora Thorne was a hedgewitch because of a hex. It was a disgrace or a tragedy, depending on which side of the hex you were on, but Rosalyn?

She was the cripple.

Rosalyn swallowed and ignored the heat in her face. "My shop, *Thornes and All,* gets a lot of customers." She was proud of how cool her voice sounded. "Lots of traders. Itinerants. People who traffic in goods legal and illicit." This was the cover story she had concocted on the way over to explain the dragon blood. What did it matter to them, how she got it? And there was no need to drag the dragon prince into this.

The receptionist went back to tending her nails. "I had no idea a hedgewitch's life was so exciting." Disdain drenched her words.

"It is when a trade for dragon blood walks into your shop."

The woman stopped fussing with her nails and blinked. Slowly, she turned the squinty glare on her. "Dragons are just a—"

Rosalyn opened her purse.

The woman's frown as she peered inside sent a rush of satisfaction through Rosalyn.

"That could be—"

"Anyone's blood?" Rosalyn smirked. "Could be. Then again, maybe it's real. Do you want Hecca to know who turned away her chance to be the first—*and only*—coven in town to get her hands on it?"

The woman's impeccably pale skin whitened just a little more.

"I didn't think so." Rosalyn gestured to the phone. "Call her."

The receptionist hesitated, then slowly stood. "Please wait just a moment." All of a sudden, her voice was practiced and professional.

It made Rosalyn want to snarl, but instead, she just gave the receptionist a nod. The woman scurried away on her supermodel legs and five-inch heels into the inner office. As Rosalyn waited, she straightened her simple white blouse and black skirt. Same outfit she'd worn before, but it was pretty much the only office-presentable clothes she owned. Someday, when she was a fully-practicing witch, she'd have all the money she needed to buy the high-fashion clothes worn by the witches of Morgan Media. Not that she actually liked that kind of thing—she was more comfortable in her jeans and t-shirt down in the shop—but if she wanted to be part of their society, she'd have to dress the part. And learn the magic. And eventually, maybe even earn their respect.

One thing was certain—they'll have never seen a witch who worked so hard. Rosalyn had a lot of years to catch up on.

She scooped her purse filled with dragon blood off the desk and held it tight. Less than a minute passed, not even enough time for Rosalyn to get jumpy, and the receptionist returned. Only she hadn't just brought Hecca Morgan with her—Circe Morgan, her sister, strode out of the inner office doors as well. Rosalyn recognized them from their online bios, but they were astonishingly more beautiful in person. It struck her mute for a moment. They were tall and poised and as voluptuous as any model in a magazine. They both had midnight-black hair that fell in lush waves to their waists, and their high, carved cheekbones definitely showed the family resemblance. Circe's eyes sparkled blue, whereas Hecca's were dark and deep.

And those eyes were trained on her like birds of prey who had found a new sparrow.

Rosalyn swallowed down her sudden inability to speak. "Thanks for seeing me." It sounded awkward. Not at all how she wanted to lead. She cleared her throat. "I have something that might interest you."

"So Lilith says." Hecca Morgan stepped forward, her slinky red dress hugging her curves. She had to be every guy's wet dream. She stopped in front of Rosalyn, towering over her. "But what would a hedgewitch be doing with dragon blood? Are you sure you haven't been swindled, my dear?" That *my dear* couldn't have been more laced with disdain.

"I know it works," Rosalyn said, the confidence in her voice swelling. This much she had down solid. "My mom's been sick. Cancer. For a while now."

Hecca frowned as Rosalyn fished out one of the vials of blood.

"I injected just half a vial of this into her… and now she's completely cured."

Hecca's impeccably-shaped eyebrows slowly hiked to the top of her forehead. "Is that right?" Then she glanced all around Rosalyn as if studying the air around her head. Rosalyn had read about this on the forums but never seen it for herself. *Aura reading.* If the emotion was strong enough, a *true witch* could see it in a person's aura. Worked on humans and witches alike.

Of course, Rosalyn couldn't see anything. But then she wasn't a *true witch.* Maybe someday…

"I see." The sharp look in Hecca's eyes suddenly seemed dangerous. She reached for the vial. "Let me take a look."

Rosalyn pulled it back. "Let's discuss my price."

Her eyes flashed, and Rosalyn tried to not let the churning of her stomach show on her face.

"The hedgewitch has a price." Hecca threw a smirk back to her sister.

Circe stepped forward, eyes wide, still examining the

aura around Rosalyn's head. "So the stories are true." She scowled at Hecca. "The dragons haven't meddled in our affairs for hundreds of years. Let's not give them a reason to start."

Meddled? Rosalyn wasn't sure what that meant, but it didn't sound good. She was even more glad she hadn't brought the dragon prince into this. As far as Morgan Media needed to know, a mysterious peddler showed up at her shop with his ill-gotten goods.

"Oh, Circe, dear." Hecca's smile was hungry as she stared at the vial. "You need to learn how to grab an opportunity when it walks in your door."

Circe scowled. "This is too dangerous."

Hecca laughed, and it chilled Rosalyn to the bone. "The dangerous part is already done." She eyed Rosalyn like she was a steak she was deciding how to carve up and eat.

Rosalyn tried to keep her voice even. "You can have all of it. All I ask is a way back in. To learn some spells. I don't even..." She glanced at Circe and the receptionist, but her proposal wasn't getting a warm reception from any of them. "I just want access to the craft. I don't even have to come into the office—"

Hecca raised a single eyebrow. "Oh, you won't need to come in *at all.*" Then her hand whipped up, and her fingers twirled in front of Rosalyn's face.

Rosalyn flinched—or she would have if she could move.

She was frozen.

Hecca's sinister smile just grew.

Oh, God. Rosalyn's heart thudded in her chest. She could only take the most shallow breaths. The rest of her body felt like it was frozen in invisible ice. A horrible shudder ran up and down her back.

Hecca snapped her fingers at the receptionist. She hopped like an electrocuted bunny over to Rosalyn's side and tried to wrench the purse full of dragon blood away from her grasp. It took a while. Rosalyn's hands were frozen in place, gripping the purse. She was terrified the woman might knock her over. For all she knew, she'd shatter into a million pieces on the sparkling granite entryway.

Finally, the purse was torn from her hands. Rosalyn would have cried if she could.

The receptionist shuffled back, smirking. The grin on Hecca's face was equally chilling. Circe was mostly scowling, as if all the protest she could muster was that this might somehow be dangerous *to the coven*. They didn't care about Rosalyn. Or her mother. They certainly weren't interested in letting her into the coven.

They just took what they wanted… because they could.

She hadn't loathed a set of witches this much since she and her mother were shoved out the door of her father's coven. And then she mostly had been terrified because she was just a kid. Now… now her hatred was all grown up, pure and sharp and honed on thousands of hours of scrabbling for a living off minor trade with witches just like these.

Witches who loathed her.

She was glad the angry tears couldn't release from her eyes.

"Let's get rid of it quickly," Circe hissed. "Use it up."

"Well, that won't work at all." Hecca scowled at her, but it was light and teasing. "How will the other covens know of our prize if we spend it all in one place?"

It was like they had forgotten about her. She was so foolish to tackle this on her own. Shame, anger, and a hot need for justice burned inside her.

"Hecca, don't be a fool!" Circe's beautiful face was marred by a scowl. "The dragons will hear of it eventually."

She shrugged. "Let them come."

Circe's scowl finally turned angry. "You'll get us all reduced to ash!" She stepped past her sister and up to Rosalyn. With a wave of her hand, Rosalyn was released. She fell to the floor. Her limbs were all buzzing with the leftover spell, not working right. She struggled to get upright. Circe's scowl was now turned on her. "Where did you get this blood, hedgewitch? I want the truth. Have you had contact with the dragons? Are they nearby? Are they a menace to our coven?"

"Oh, for the love of magic, Circe!" Hecca's sarcasm dripped. "She's a *hedgewitch.* She's not consorting with dragons."

But Circe's blazing blue eyes didn't leave Rosalyn's face. "Do you know where they are?"

"No." Rosalyn tried not to squirm under the intensity of the witch's stare.

But then Circe scanned the air above Rosalyn's head, and her heart skipped a beat.

"She's lying." Circe whipped a glare back to her sister. *"Hecca."*

Oh no.

Her sister's perfectly shaped lips were pressed together, studying the mysterious aura above Rosalyn's head. *It was betraying her.* Then Hecca flicked a manicured finger her way. "Bring her inside."

"Wait! I can explain." Rosalyn's heart was spasming so hard it was cutting off all her air.

The receptionist stalked up to her with a maniacal glint in her eye. "Oh, you'll explain all right, hedgewitch." She gritted her teeth. "Do you want to walk or be dragged?"

Rosalyn swallowed. Circe and Hecca were already heading back inside the warren of cubicles and offices. Rosalyn could try to run, but one of them would just turn her into a living popsicle. Her feet almost refused to move, but she forced them forward, step by slow step.

She was entering the Morgan coven… but not at all the way she planned.

Chapter Thirteen

Leonidas landed, shifted, and barreled into Rosalyn's shop.

He was moving so fast, he nearly ripped the decrepit door off its hinges. Fixing that could wait—Rosalyn's safety couldn't.

There was no one in the front of the shop.

"Rosalyn!" he called out as he ran toward the back. "Where are you?" He was breathless, and his voice hitched up with panic.

"She's not here," said a feminine voice from behind the beaded curtain, but it didn't belong to Rosalyn. Leonidas reached the doorway just as Rosalyn's mother did, nearly mowing the woman down.

He jerked back, then gripped the frame of the door to anchor himself and keep from charging through the back, demanding to see her. Because every fiber of his being wanted to do exactly that. He'd been in a panic all the way from the keep, and the adrenaline was amping him up… and bringing out his dragon in a way that was *not* controlled.

He needed to calm the fuck down.

"Where is she, Ms. Thorne?" he said, breath heaving. He was still fighting an internal war to keep that *wildness* at bay. If his wyvern wanted to come out and end all of this insanity, *fine*. But Leonidas would damn well make sure Rosalyn was safe first.

She frowned. "Why are you here?" Despite the suspicious look she was giving him, she was the picture of health—nothing like the aged woman he saw when he was here last, drinking poisoned tea. Back then, he thought she was just elderly, but clearly, it had only been the disease ravaging her body. Now her cheeks were flushed with good health, and her eyes were bright.

And wary.

"I'm concerned about her," Leonidas rushed out, then grimaced. How much should he tell Rosalyn's mother? The most important thing was finding Rosalyn quickly… "Look, I don't know what she's told you, but—"

She held up a hand to stop him, then gave it a brief, amazed glance. Like she couldn't quite believe the vibrancy of her own skin. Her green eyes then drilled into his. "She told me you're a dragon. And that you gave her your blood to cure me." She smiled a little, but it was tight. "Whatever you expect from my daughter in exchange—"

"*No.*" His intensity startled her—hell, it startled *him.* "It's not like that," he rushed out. "It's… complicated. I'll explain everything later, I promise, but right now, I'm concerned for Rosalyn's safety. *Please.* Just tell me where I can find her."

Her suspicious look muted somewhat, shoved out by the concern that flooded it. "How is she in danger?"

Leonidas gritted his teeth to keep his frustration inside. *This was taking too long.* So he went for the quickest explanation. "Look, there are demons in Seattle. Vampires as well.

I'm a *dragon*, Ms. Thorne—it's my job to keep these things out of the human population. So, obviously, I'm fucking up in that regard. But more importantly, I think they might be targeting Rosalyn. I need to find her and make sure she's safe."

As he spoke, her eyes went wider, and a worried scowl settled in. "All these things… are they because of *you?* Did you bring this into her life?"

He physically cringed. Because there was only one answer to that. "Yes. And I need to make it right."

Her eyes narrowed, appraising, but she quickly gave him a nod. "I don't know much about dragons, but I know a thing or two about shifters. And if you're anything like…" She blinked, hesitated just a fraction of a second, then said, "She took your blood to a coven downtown. Morgan Media."

He grimaced. "I was afraid of that."

"I told her not to." The woman's scowl was back. "She doesn't know those witches like I do. But she wouldn't listen."

He nodded, but he was already itching to take flight and go after her. "I'll bring her back, safe and sound, Ms. Thorne. I promise."

She shook her head. "I'll go with you. I can get you inside and—"

"*No.*" Frustration was causing his talons to come out. "I'm sorry, just… trust me, a few witches won't be a problem. And besides…" He gave her a tight smile. "Flying is faster."

Her eyes widened, but he didn't wait, just turned and sprinted toward the front door. As soon as he cleared the shop, he cloaked, shifted, and launched himself into the air. The Morgan coven operated out of a high-rise downtown, and while the House of Smoke hadn't made contact

in hundreds of years, he definitely knew where it was—
even before his recent inquiries under the guise of a wolf
had refreshed his memory of all the coven locations. It
took no time to get there, and even as he dipped down to
fly into the parking garage and startled an office worker by
seemingly appearing out of nowhere, he was reaching with
his fae senses to the thirty-fifth floor. He couldn't sense any
demons or vampires, but the thick, magic-sparking pres-
ence of the coven made it difficult to pinpoint Rosalyn's
location. He believed her mother, though—she *had* to be
there. She was trading his blood for the one thing she really
wanted—to become a true witch, attaining the full glory of
all her powers.

As the elevator rose, guilt stabbed him, and agitation
rode him hard. He would barrel in on whatever negotiations she had going and probably screw all that up for her.
But he *had* to make sure she was safe—after that, he could
repair the damage.

The Morgan coven may not have seen a dragon for
centuries, but their elders had to have passed the stories
down, warning them not to mess with the gatekeepers of
the immortal realm.

And if they hadn't… well, he would set them straight.

The elevator finally ended its torturously slow ascent.
He strode quickly to the frosted glass doors of Morgan
Media and pulled them open.

The receptionist seemed startled to see him. "Can I
help you?"

"No." He headed straight for the interior doors,
reaching ahead and searching for Rosalyn. He found her in
the east corner of the building with several other witches,
her unique lavender-and-berries flavor standing out.

"Sir, you can't just—" The receptionist threw minor
magic at him.

He batted it away then pushed open the frosted glass doors, pausing only to throw a quick glare to her. "Don't."

He left her open-mouthed behind him and marched into the open office area. A rustle of concern and a crackling of magical energy followed him toward the east corner. He ignored all of it—the stares and whispers as well—in his single-minded focus on reaching Rosalyn. But as he drew closer, something was off about her taste—the potent energy of her magic was dulled somehow.

He burst into the room, and his anger flared.

Rosalyn was in a chair, surrounded by three witches. Her head was hanging down, her red hair falling forward to obscure her face, but she was mumbling something, her voice slurred, almost drunken.

The witches snapped their attention to him. One fell back, hiding behind Rosalyn's chair. The other two—tall and imposing, with faces he vaguely recognized as part of the Morgan lineage—fell into defensive stances. The one with blazing dark eyes took the lead, while the other stepped back with a fearful look. The dark-eyed Morgan witch quickly flicked her wrist to conjure a seething blue ball of energy. Before she could fling it at him, he used his fae magic to lift the fireball from her control. He sent it crashing into the carpet at the foot of the blue-eyed Morgan witch, the one holding back with a fearful look. She yelped and jumped back further.

"Never fight a dragon with fire," he said coolly.

Fury blazed on the leader's face. "Who the hell do you think you are? *Get out.*" She brought both hands forward in a sudden clap, releasing a pulse of magic that swept through the room. It bounced harmlessly off him, but reflected off the walls as well, and he had to grab hold of the energy and redirect it before it sliced a burn across Rosalyn in her chair. He sent it crashing into the heavy wooden desk next to her. It smoldered, like the carpet behind her.

Enough of this shit.

Leonidas sucked in a breath and roared, releasing a plume of dragonfire. He focused it on the enormously ostentatious desk, which was already smoking from the witch's fireball, and engulfed it in a blaze of blue. In less than a second, the entire thing was consumed, reduced to a feathery pile of gray ash.

"Do *not* fuck with the House of Smoke," he said, but the three witches were already cowering away from the inferno. It blazed up then quickly quenched as it ran out of things to burn, all in the span of a second.

Rosalyn's attention was finally drawn to the destruction of the desk. "Wow," she said in a drunken voice that wrenched his heart. *What did they do to her?* "That's a lot of fire. Ha! Fire… fire from the dragon prince…" Her head lolled to the side, a sloppy grin on her face as her gaze wandered the room, apparently looking for the witches. "I told you he was *hot.*" Then she giggled like a little girl.

Leonidas stumbled forward and knelt by her chair. She seemed unharmed, and nothing was binding her to the seat—real or magical. She was just intoxicated or under some kind of spell. He took her hands and guided her up to standing.

"Oh!" She couldn't quite stand on her own, so he caught her around the waist to hold her up. Her head banged forward on his chest then rolled to the side. She mumbled something, then lifted her head and squinted at him. "You're so *big.* And sexy. *Sooooo* sexy." She patted his chest. "I didn't *want* to tell them, dragon prince." She shook her head. "Nope. Didn't want to. But I couldna dinna help it. Nope."

He grimaced as he reached a hand to her cheek,

summoning his runes and his healing magic to banish whatever spell they had put her under. He could taste the bitterness of it even as it fled her mind and her body. He pumped extra magic in, just in case.

It was like she suddenly woke up. "Whoa." She blinked and pushed away from him.

He reluctantly released her.

Now her eyes were sharp, but they filled with a fear that tore into him. "I tried not to tell them. *I swear,*" she said. "I just couldn't—"

He held up a hand to stop her. "Are you okay?" He was scanning her with his fae senses, but he could find no trace of the spell remaining.

Her eyes went a little wider, but she nodded.

"*I told you,*" whispered one of the witches, the blue-eyed one.

The dark-eyed one's stare was fixed on him. "We didn't know she was your special plaything, dragon."

Rosalyn tensed but kept silent.

Anger seethed in his chest. So it was okay to spell-drug Rosalyn as long as there wasn't someone bigger and badder—namely *him*—there to stop them. "She is under my protection," he said, just to make that perfectly clear.

The dark-eyed Morgan witch tipped her head. "Understood."

"And you have something of mine." He could taste the magical trace of his own blood in the room—it sat on the shelf next to the chair, still in Rosalyn's leather purse. He lifted his chin to Rosalyn then gestured to the purse. "It belongs to you. Go get it."

She frowned but hurried over to retrieve it, then held the purse to her chest like she would protect it with her life. He beckoned her over with a wave of his hand.

She glowered but came to stand by his side.

"I need you to come with me right now," he said to her, softly, peering into those beautiful blue eyes. "We can sort out the rest of this later." He turned back to the Morgan witches. "It's been a while since the House of Smoke felt it necessary to step into your realm. The coven of Morgan used to be a respectable practitioner of the dark arts. Have you sunk so low that you now torment your own?" He let his scorn ring clear. "Are you so greedy for magic that you can't accept a new witch into your fold without tormenting her for more?"

"That *hedgewitch* isn't one of ours," the dark-eyed one said. She was as haughty as any witch Leonidas had met. The epitome of what he thought all witches were, with the exceptions of Meridi and now Rosalyn. That Rosalyn wanted to be one of them made him cringe inside. But she deserved to know her powers, and this was something he could arrange. Force it, as apparently he must. Like Cinaed said, he had that power. And he would wield it for her, to right the wrong done to her so long ago.

"And yet," Leonidas said, with a glance for the desk he had just reduced to ash, "I'm sure you could find room in your hearts for another sister in your coven. If the House of Smoke requested it."

Rosalyn sucked in a breath. "Leonidas, *no.*"

He flicked a look to her—the anger on her face knocked him back.

"Of course, if the House of Smoke made a special request," the dark-eyed Morgan witch said with far too much purr in her voice. A calculating glint had taken up residence in her eyes. "And perhaps a steady supply of dragon blood to enhance our operations?"

"Don't push it, witch," he growled. But it was the terrified look on Rosalyn's face that concerned him. He needed to talk to her—*alone.* Away from the prying eyes of this den of snakes called a coven. He reached for Rosalyn's elbow and guided her toward the door. To the Morgan witch, he said, "You'll be hearing from me. In the meantime, watch your step, coven of Morgan."

The dark-eyed witch glared, but her blue-eyed sister held her back with a hand on her arm and a shake of her head.

Leonidas led Rosalyn out of the office, back through the warren of cubicles and passing through the entranceway. They didn't speak again until they reached the elevators.

Leonidas pushed the button to summon it. "You have to come back to the keep," he said, quietly, glancing back at the closed doors of Morgan Media. "It's not safe for you in Seattle right now."

"*What?* No. I'm not coming back, Leonidas." The fearful look was back on her face.

He grimaced. "It's just temporary," he tried to reassure her, but it didn't seem to work. He gestured to the giant glass wall behind them. "We can come back here later. I'll get you into the coven then."

"*No!* God! Just…" She clutched her purse and edged away from him. "Just stay out of my life."

"I'm not trying to—"

The elevator dinged, and the door opened. He bit his tongue and gestured for her to go first. She stepped into the elevator, but her body was stiff like she was expecting the elevator ride to be some kind of trap.

When the door closed again, he said, "Someone's targeting the women who answered the WildLove ad. *Hunting them.* I'm not sure exactly what's happening but…" He drifted off at the look on her face. Suspicion. Fear. Her back was up against the side of the elevator, clutching her purse to her chest.

It was wrenching his stomach.

"Are you..." she started, then stopped. "Is this just some way to get me back there? To the keep? So you can hold me prisoner?"

"What? No!" *For the love of magic...* he was ready to tear out his hair with this.

"Then just leave me alone." She turned to stare at the quickly counting down numbers of the elevator.

"Rosalyn." He edged closer, even though she was giving off body signals about as hostile as a drone strike. "I can get you into the coven. I know that's what you want—"

"You don't know *anything* about me." She squinted her anger at him. "You don't get it, do you? Those witches... I have to *earn* my way in, Leonidas. Otherwise, it will never work."

He frowned, and she was right—he didn't get it. "If I ask them—"

"If you *threaten them,* you mean." She was breathing through her teeth. "What do you think will happen once you fly back to your keep? Your perfect palace hidden away in the mountains? I'll be *ash* before you can say *fuck you, hedgewitch.*"

That both stabbed him and made him angry. Burn-down-a-coven angry. "Not if those witches value their lives."

"Right," she said, huffing a laugh. Her bitterness baffled him. "And what then, dragon prince? Are you going to burn down every coven in Seattle? What happens to my shop? My mom? *Thornes and All* will be blackballed. *Ruined.* I've worked too hard... I've worked too long..." Her eyes were glassing up, and it was ripping a hole in Leonidas's gut.

The door of the elevator slid open.

"If you want to help me," she hissed low, so the hapless

office workers outside the elevator wouldn't be startled, "then stay the hell away." She turned her back on him and stalked out of the elevator and toward the door of the high-rise. He followed her but stopped in the atrium of the building, watching her hurry away.

She didn't want his help. *Refused* to let him help her. *Fuck.* He couldn't even do this right. But there was no way in hell he was letting her roam Seattle unprotected.

She just needed time to calm down. To think things over. She'd just been assaulted and turned away from the coven she'd been trying to buy her way into, for magic's sake.

She was upset. He could give her time.

But he'd be watching over her every second.

He waited until she left the building to start following her. It was easy enough to track her magical lavender scent. Once he was outside, he ducked into an alley, shifted and cloaked and went aloft. She was taking a bus across downtown. A hundred people surrounded her—on the bus, on the street—but none were vamps or demons, at least as much as he could tell. The demons especially concerned him. They were damned hard to detect, only showing their essence when the evil inside them rose up. But he was close enough he could swoop down and snatch her away from harm with just a moment's notice.

He circled the city street, hovering above her bus, waiting. Watching.

When she was ready, he'd try again.

Chapter Fourteen

*H*OLY *FUCKING MAGIC*, THIS DAY.

Rosalyn was barely holding it together. Once she was on the bus, the shakes really set in. An old guy, homeless by the looks of it, was watching her warily, like he thought she was hyped up on some kind of drug and therefore danger-ous. But clearly, she wasn't a threat to much of anyone.

Hedgewitch.

The name had implanted in her brain like a horrible weed.

She'd tried to buy her way into a coven and ended up just another pawn in their witching games. More power. More greed. More magic. As if they didn't have *all the magic* already! If Leonidas hadn't interrupted them, she might never have gotten out of there. She knew that, but she'd been so shaken, so angry, so *devastated* by everything having gone sideways… she just couldn't let him waltz in and try to fix things. Or sweep her off to his keep again. Trap her in a haze of sexual pleasure until he convinced her to do whatever he wanted—make dragon babies, she guessed, although why he couldn't just fucking find someone else for that, she didn't know.

Everything was ruined.

She wiped angrily at the tears trickling down her face.

At least her mom was healed. She had the dragon prince to thank for that, and she really should do that at some point. She'd already thanked him once, but here he was, saving her from the mess she was in *again...* and she didn't manage to say thank you before she ran the hell out of there. At least, he let her go. *Mental note*—thank the dragon at some point. Not now. Not while he was still bent on getting her back to the keep. That story about someone stalking the women who showed up to date him was over the top. And offering to force the Morgan sisters to take her? *Holy magic,* that would have been a disaster. Maybe he was just getting desperate. Maybe he was near the end and had to mate like *tomorrow* or something.

Who knew what was going on with him.

It wasn't her problem.

Her problem was where to go from here.

She was sitting in a bus, rumbling down the grimy end of Seattle, but where was she really going? She still had the dragon blood. She might do something with that. Maybe just keep it and dole it out to her mom over time? That might be as good as the health spells she would learn as a true witch. How did you even store blood? Did it go bad after a while? She had no clue. The Morgan sisters might come after her, even though Leonidas did a good job of scaring the crap out of them. A bitter smile wrenched out of her, but it was quickly followed by the threat of more tears. There was no hope of joining the Morgan coven now.

Everything had gone so far wrong.

She rubbed her face with both hands then sucked in a deep breath.

There was nothing to do but go home, check in with her mom, and regroup. The two of them had scraped through everything over the years—they'd figure this out, too. Her mom still hated the witching community for banishing her, so Rosalyn had never brought up her secret plans to get back inside until today. And it turned into exactly the ugly fight she's always imagined. But she might change that. Maybe between her mom and Aunt Alora—assuming she could get the two together on this—could both help her figure out where to go from here.

It wasn't much of a plan, but it was all she could put together in her freaked-out state by the time the bus arrived at her stop. The shakes were mostly gone, and as she climbed down from the bus and strode fast to her shop, her heart settled a little more. It was like any other day, coming home from scavenging herbs or scouting antiquities stores downtown. She would go settle in, have a long talk and maybe some peppermint tea with her mom, and they'd figure this all out.

Together.

Rosalyn strode up the shop… but the door was open. Not just open—it had been ripped off its hinges and barely hung on by the last nail.

A gush of dread iced her stomach. "Mom?" she called out, hurrying inside. There was nothing wrong with the shop that she could see. She dropped her purse on one of the tables and hustled to the back, plunging through the beaded curtain—

There was some guy kissing the hell out of her mother.

Rosalyn just stood and stared. The guy was big and toned but not too muscular in his rumpled suit. He had her mom bent backward in one of those Hollywood-type kisses, giving her a hickey on her neck while her mom's arms lay limp at her sides. She was kind of moaning with it, too, which was just gross. Technically, she guessed her mom was free to date or make out or whatever, but in reality, she never did. Maybe the miracle cure made her want to run out and hook up with the next weirdo who waltzed into their shop.

Rosalyn cleared her throat. "Excuse me—"

The guy whipped around. *Holy fuck.* His lips were smeared with blood. Her mom… there was blood on her neck… *what the hell?*

Rosalyn grabbed the shop broom by the doorway and screamed, "Get away from her, you fucker!" as she charged him. His arms were still full with holding her mother's limp body, so Rosalyn got in a good hit, right on the back of his head. But he didn't go down, just cringed away and dropped her mother—she landed with a sickening thud on the concrete floor. Rosalyn wanted to go to her, but the guy recovered too quickly. He growled and lunged toward her. Rosalyn let out a yelp and swung the broom again, but he was ready this time, jerking back as it whizzed past his head, then grabbing hold of it and yanking her off her feet. His clammy hands were on her, pulling her close. The broom was between them, and she fought against him, but he was strong—too strong for such a lean build. And his face was so pale. And his eyes, now that he was close… they were all black. One hundred percent pupil except for a thin red line around the edge. He was some kind of monster. A blood-sucking monster. *Vampire,* the small, terrified part of her mind screeched. He was winning the fight to reach her neck, and as his mouth opened, she saw two needle-sharp fangs inside…

She screamed.

But just as she felt the twin pricks sink into her skin—the monster was ripped away.

He sailed through the air like a puppet that weighed nothing. A roar filled her ears, and a blur rushed after the vampire. *Leonidas.* A tumble of boxes crashed down from the shelves onto the creature. Leonidas pushed them aside to haul the crumpled vampire up from the floor. Leonidas's hand had changed into giant razor-sharp talons that encircled the creature's neck. Even Rosalyn could see that struggling against *that* would cut off its head.

With the vampire pinned in place, Leonidas whipped around, his gaze hunting for her. His blue eyes flashed bronze, which was both beautiful and chilling. "Are you all right?" he asked her, hoarsely.

"Yes." She nodded to back it up, but a trickle along her neck itched, and it came away bloody.

"You're *bleeding,*" he accused, then he stomped across the floor, dragging the vampire with him. The creature was clutching at Leonidas's wrist to keep from being decapitated.

"Don't kill me!" the vampire gasped.

"Shut up," Leonidas spat at him, but when he reached Rosalyn, his expression was nothing but tormented concern. "Let me…" He reached for her neck. The runes she'd seen on his body during all their lovemaking skittered down his arm and piled up on his hand. What small amount of pain throbbed at her neck instantly ceased.

A moan behind Leonidas reminded her… "My mom!" Rosalyn scooted around the flailing vampire and Leonidas's deadly talons and ran to kneel by her mother, who was just working her way up to sitting and holding her head.

"What was… Rosalyn?" Her mother peered at her like she wasn't sure if her daughter was a dream. There was blood all over her neck, and her mother's face was three shades too pale.

"Dragon prince!" Rosalyn beseeched, her throat closing up, but Leonidas was already right behind her.

He dropped the vampire on the floor and put his foot on the creature's neck, pinning him. "Don't move," he said, then turned to Rosalyn's mother. He reached for her neck, but her mother shied away, flailing her hands in front of her face like they didn't quite work.

"It's okay, Mom," Rosalyn said past the lump in her throat. "Leonidas can help."

Her mother frowned, and her eyes seemed glazed, but she let Leonidas put his palm to her neck.

"You're going to be okay," he said, his voice soothing, and Rosalyn could kiss him just for that. But even better, whatever he was doing, it was bringing a sharper focus to her mom's eyes and a flush back to her skin. Rosalyn gingerly touched where he had healed her neck. Was there no end to this dragon prince's magic? If the most powerful witches bowed before him… she was just now beginning to understand the scope of his power. Or maybe beginning to realize she *didn't* understand. Not at all. That he was helping her *once again* brought the lump back to her throat.

Then he frowned. "What the…"

Those two words sent a chill through her. "What's wrong?"

"It's… fine." But the runes were racing up and down his arm to the hand he still held to her mother's throat. He focused intently on them. Rosalyn was about to ask again, demand he tell her, but he dropped his hand from her mom's neck and spoke directly to her. "You didn't lose too much blood, Ms. Thorne. We must have caught the vampire early in his feed."

"Is that what he is?" she asked, blinking and dazed and

casting a fearful glance at the vampire still pinned under Leonidas's foot. "I… I guess I don't know how long he… *fed.*" She looked a little sick to her stomach.

"You're going to be fine," Leonidas said again, and Rosalyn felt the tension loosen in her shoulders. She believed him. And it seemed like her mom did as well. "I've sealed the puncture wound, but more importantly, I've pumped some healing magic in you to rev up the dragon blood you already have circulating inside. That regenerates quickly, so you should be back to full speed, soon. If not…" Leonidas glanced at Rosalyn. "I believe your daughter still has a few vials that should more than suffice."

Rosalyn nodded to confirm that. And she was suddenly glad to have it, rather than having bargained it away.

"Why don't you get your mom to bed? She should rest." Leonidas looked back to the vampire still splayed flat on the floor. "I'm going to take out the trash." The dragon prince stood, then reached down to haul the vampire off the floor. It was as if the creature weighed nothing.

"No, please don't… please don't kill me…" The begging was pathetic, but then again, Rosalyn wasn't at all sure what Leonidas had planned. As he dragged the stumbling vampire toward the back door, Rosalyn hurried to help her mother up. She was pretty spritely—Rosalyn still wasn't used to her being in such good health. Even with a vampire attack, she was still moving faster than she was before, with the cancer eating away at her whole system. Rosalyn still held her elbow because she seemed unsteady, woozy from the attack.

"I'm really fine," her mother said with a small smile as Rosalyn escorted her to her room. "But I'll lie down for a little bit. Give you two time to talk." Then she frowned. "Please make sure that *thing* doesn't come back." Rosalyn was sure she meant the vampire, not Leonidas. Her mom visibly shuddered, then made her way to the bed in the corner. Rosalyn stayed until she made it safely across the room, then she hurried out to the back.

Leonidas was interrogating the vampire… by means of fisting his shirt in one hand and slamming him up against the wall with his feet dangling below. "What the hell were you doing to her?"

Rosalyn caught the terrified vampire's gaze, and Leonidas grimaced when he realized she was watching.

But he just shifted his other hand into talons—the one not holding the vampire up against the wall. "Answer me."

"I just wanted a taste, I swear." The vampire was shaking as he answered.

Rosalyn didn't know if she cared if Leonidas killed this creature—he attacked her mom—but she *did* want to know what he meant. Wasn't it obvious the vampire was after her mom's blood? And then hers? Or was there something else? She was barely wrapping her brain around the fact that vampires *existed*, for fuck's sake.

Rosalyn edged up to Leonidas. "What's going on?" she asked, softly. He didn't owe her anything. She owed *him*, big time. But this whole thing was freaking her out.

He glared at the vampire then turned a softer frown to her. "I told you—the women who answered the ad are being targeted. One was drained, by fuckers like this one." He slammed the vampire against the wall again, and the thing whimpered.

It made her cringe, even though she hated it for what it tried to do. *Drained.* It gave her the shudders.

"But another one was demon infected," Leonidas said, more softly this time.

Rosalyn leaned back. "Demons? Like… real demons?" Her world was turning inside out. She knew about magic, but it was all ordinary magic. Shifter magic. Witching magic. Spells and casting and hexes and potions. Demons were… that was heaven and hell type stuff. A whole different realm.

"Yes, they're very real," Leonidas said, bitterly. "Demons staged an attack on the keep not long ago. My father, the king, was poisoned by one of the demon-infected mercenaries who overran us." She could hear the pain in his voice.

Rosalyn didn't know what to say. "I'm sorry," she mumbled. It seemed wholly inadequate.

"They've been popping up in the human population for a while," Leonidas pressed on. "We didn't know why, but then one of the women was infected, and now this…" He glared at the vampire again. "This *trash* was somehow demon-infecting your mother."

Rosalyn's eyes flew wide. "My mother's a demon?" She glanced in horror back at the open back door of her shop. *No.* She refused to believe it.

"*No,*" Leonidas said, emphatically. "At least, not anymore. But when I visited your mother just before going to the coven, she had no sign of demon infection. When I came back, she was filled with demon essence. It *had* to be him. But it's okay now. I cured her."

Rosalyn gaped at him. "You can do that?"

A bitter smile curved up one corner of his lips. "You don't know anything about me, Rosalyn Thorne."

His words struck her like a hammer to the chest, knocking the air straight out of her body. Because they were *her* words… *and he was right.* She knew nothing about him.

"I know you're a really good man, Leonidas Smoke." It was the least she could say for all he'd done. She was losing count of the ways he had saved her and her mom.

Her words seemed to stun him, and he searched her face for a moment. The bronze flashed in his eyes again, and it mesmerized her, but he quickly turned away, hiding his face and staring at the floor. "I'm not as good as you think," he whispered. At least, she thought he said that. It was so quiet. He cleared his throat and looked up again. "The important thing is to get you and your mom to safety." Then he turned a snarl back to the vampire. "And *you* get to tell me how you did it. How you infected her mother with demon essence. Or you can die in this stinking alley. Believe me, it would give me great pleasure to feel your infernal blood running over my talons."

"Please." The vampire held up his hands. "If I tell you, they'll kill me."

"The fae." It was a statement.

The fae? What in the world was he talking about?

"Winter court or summer?" Leonidas asked.

The man grimaced but said nothing.

Leonidas held up his hand with the six-inch talons.

Holy crap, those things looked deadly.

"Okay, okay," the vampire said, hastily. "Winter Court. They've found a loophole. A way around the treaty. A way to conjure demons without breaking it."

"Keep talking," Leonidas said when it seemed like the vampire was having second thoughts. Rosalyn didn't know what treaty he was talking about, but she kept quiet. It was obvious there was a *lot* she didn't know.

"The fae gave us something *extra* in our venom," the vampire said, slowly, like each word of admission was costing him. "I don't know what it is—it's fucking fae magic, okay?—but if you undergo the treatment, your venom changes. It's not just the intoxicant, anymore, the pleasure anesthetizer. They add some kind of forgetting magic. We can feed all we want, and they never remember it. And when we do, we leave something else behind. Something that alters their DNA. I don't know how the magic works, but after I feed, they're demons. It doesn't take long, either, so whatever it is, it's flipping them fast. The fae explained to my coven leader that it wasn't violating the treaty because it wasn't actually harming the humans. It was making them stronger, and they'd live longer, too. It just *changed* them. Brought out their inner demon, or whatever. I don't know." He looked fearful again. "But it doesn't violate the treaty, okay? I mean, if it did, you'd feel it, right? We'd all feel it."

Leonidas snarled at that, but then he released the vampire.

The thing sagged down the wall, his boots landing roughly on the ground. "*Fuck,*" he spat. "The fae are going to kill me."

Rosalyn gave Leonidas a wide-eyed look. Was he just letting the vampire go?

"If I catch you infecting anyone else," Leonidas said, giving him a cool look, "I'll cut off your head and ask questions later."

The vampire's hand went reflexively to his neck, which was reddened from their altercation.

"Go back to your coven," Leonidas continued. "Tell the rest we're watching for them. If they come to the city, or anywhere near humans, their lifetimes are going to be severely shortened. And if the attacks don't stop, we'll come hunt you down wherever you are."

The vampire grimaced but nodded. Then he shuffled away down the alley, picking up speed as he went.

Leonidas turned back to her. "Please tell me you'll come to the keep. You and your mother both. We don't have to…" He gestured between the two of them. "There doesn't have to be anything between us. I just need to know you're safe."

"Okay," Rosalyn said.

He leaned back and cocked an eyebrow. "Okay? Just… *okay?* You're not going to fight me on this?"

"No." She felt suddenly bashful. Like she should thank him for saving her life and her mother's life, as well as saving them from some horrible fate—turning into demons, for fuck's sake—that she didn't even know was in the realm of possibilities. Somehow, all the *thank yous* in her head sounded completely inadequate for that. Instead, she asked one of the questions burning in her mind. "What's this treaty you two were talking about?"

He gave her a little, perplexed look, like he was still stunned she agreed to come under his protection, for real this time. Then he just shook his head. "It's a ten-thousand-year-old treaty that's supposed to keep the peace between the mortal and immortal realms. And keep demons away from the human population. Although, the fucking fae seem to have found a loophole around that."

"I don't understand who the fae are, but… why are they coming after the women you're dating?" Was he dating other women besides her? She had just assumed she was the only one, with the way he wouldn't leave her alone, but now she wondered… if others were being attacked… that bothered her more than it should.

He ducked his head and seemed embarrassed. "I don't need a mate just to extend my somewhat questionable existence." He peered at her with those sexy blue eyes. She couldn't quite believe she was thinking about him that way again, but with the softness in them, and the way he was looking at her like she was *important* to him, she couldn't help it. And he obviously felt bad about lying to her, when she'd lied to him every single step of the way.

It struck her hard. Leonidas may be a dragon, and she may be a defunct witch, but there was no question that he was a better *person* than she was.

Much better.

"I have to produce a dragonling to fulfill the treaty," Leonidas was saying. "At first, we thought just my brother Lucian would have to do it. We're triplets, my two brothers and I, and Lucian was first born. But once he and his mate had their dragonling, the treaty still didn't renew."

"What do you mean, it didn't renew?" she asked, eyes wide. Her mind was suddenly hungry to learn everything she could about this magical world she didn't even know existed. "Is there some kind of Dragon Supreme Court that decides these things?"

He smiled, and the smile grew, and then finally he gave a small laugh. "Oh, Rosalyn Thorne." A gleam in his eye was suddenly heating her lady parts. "You really need to stop doing that."

"Doing *what?*" She frowned. She had the distinct sense he was laughing at her.

But then he bit his lip and eased closer. Her heart thudded. Was he going to kiss her? He leaned forward... but just to kiss her on the forehead. "Charming me," he said softly. When he pulled back, that fascinating bronze color was flashing in his blue eyes again. He cleared his throat, and his smirk gentled to a soft smile. "When the treaty renews, everyone in the immortal world will feel it. It's a magical pulse that will flash through that space where magic lives. I'll tell you all about it." He dipped his head. "On the way back to the keep."

"Deal."

He smiled, a genuine one, and it reached inside her and stirred things around.

She needed to find a way to thank this dragon prince.
Soon.

Chapter Fifteen

"IT'S A GOOD THING YOU'RE A GUY, LITTLE GUY."

Leonidas was speaking, ostensibly, to the ridiculously cute baby in his arms, his nephew Larik, but his mama, Arabella, was looking on approvingly. And it was true. This kid won his heart the moment he was born. Leonidas would have been a goner had his brother's dragonling been a girl. *Thank magic,* that was an incredibly rare occurrence… and it had never happened in the House of Smoke.

"He loves you, too," Arabella said with a wide grin.

Leonidas squinted at her. "He's a baby. He loves clean diapers and his mama."

Her smile tempered a little, and she scooted closer to peer over his shoulder. "See how he's staring up at you with those big green eyes? And how his hands are relaxed and open? That means he loves looking at you." She patted Leonidas's arm, the one cradling her infant son. "I think he senses you're a dragon."

That made Leonidas lean back to see if she was joking. But she seemed deadly serious. "You think he's using his baby fae senses?" That put a whole new wonder in his brain with this dragonling business. How could something so small be so amazing? And so light—Leonidas could barely feel the weight of the tiny bundle in his arms, as if the baby were made of pure magic. He peered at little Larik. "What do you think, bud? Are we friends? We dragons have to stick together, you know."

"Knock that shit off," Lucian grumbled, returning to the great room of Leonidas's lair after finishing up his phone call with Leksander in the other room. They were making sure the women were all squared away in the keep. "You're making my mate cry."

Leonidas gave him a look like he was losing his marbles, but then Arabella stepped back and dipped her head, wiping away at something that looked a lot like tears.

"What?" he asked, mystified. Then again, the baby was so damn cute it nearly brought him to tears, too.

"Are you trying to horn in on my family here, bro?" Lucian scowled at him.

"What?" Leonidas asked again. He was lost.

Lucian looked tortured for a moment, then busted out laughing. He clapped a heavy hand on Leonidas's shoulder, jostling him.

Leonidas shrugged him off. "Hey! Holding a baby here. Watch it."

Lucian grinned just like Arabella had. "They don't break that easy."

Leonidas was starting to think that having a dragonling had done something to his brother's brain. He looked back to Larik, but somehow the magic staring spell had been broken—the little guy had fallen asleep. His hands were balled into tiny fists tucked up under his chin, and the wide-eyed wonder was replaced with a sweet closed-eyed innocence even angels couldn't beat. Not that real angels were particularly sweet *or* innocent.

"This son of yours is going to slay some hearts when he's grown," Leonidas said as he gazed at Larik. He tried to picture him as a grown man, but his brain just couldn't go there. And he was unlikely to see it in real life. He looked to Lucian. "Tell him Uncle Leonidas said to stay clear of the witches."

Lucian's expression darkened. "Tell him yourself."

Leonidas just shook his head. *Not going to happen.* But he kept that to himself. Instead, he said, "So what's the status? Did you find a place for each of the women?"

Lucian grimaced. "Yeah… about that…"

Leonidas frowned. "Please tell me you found them all."

"Oh, that. Yeah. Definitely. Leksander brought the last one in just a few minutes ago. No more casualties. Whoever hacked the WildLove app to get the data on the women who answered the post wasn't able to get to them before we were."

Leonidas raised an eyebrow. "Then what?"

The grimace was back. "We don't have enough guest room capacity for that many people. So we ended up pairing them with dragons. Each woman with an unmated member of the House of Smoke. So…"

Leonidas chuckled, trying to contain it and not jostle the baby too much. "So there's going to be a lot more sex happening in the keep very soon."

Lucian looked pained. "I've ordered them to keep their damn hands to themselves. We're supposed to be finding *you* a mate."

Leonidas shook his head. "Let them. I'm not going to make this work, Lucian. And if I do… I don't care if they've slept with someone else."

"Even Rosalyn?" His brother was nailing him with his amber-eyed stare.

Leonidas's heart lurched. "What? Wait… I thought she was staying in the main guest apartment with her mother." The idea of Rosalyn bedding down with any of the unmated dragons in the House of Smoke suddenly had his face steaming hot.

Lucian was nodding in a knowing way that was irritating as hell. "She is. Unless you want me to move her—"

"*No.*" The force of it jostled the baby, but Larik just made a little twitching movement with his nose and went back to sleep. Leonidas lowered his voice. "No, and fuck you for asking," he said in his most polite voice.

Lucian scowled. "That's what I thought. You know, we don't have to keep her here, my brother. If it's too much for you."

"It's not. I'm fine." He stared that conviction into his brother's eyes even if he didn't entirely believe it himself. Rosalyn *was* trouble for him—saving her from the witches and then that vampire had nearly brought out his wyvern —but he had it under control. Mostly. "Besides, she's not *the one*, Lucian. She has her own reasons, but they pretty much preclude falling in love with a dragon prince of the House of Smoke."

Lucian looked like he was fighting a smirk. "I'll tell Leksander she's out of the running then."

Leonidas curled up a lip. "You're really not as funny as you think."

Lucian let the smirk grow. He opened his mouth to say something probably equally stupid, but he was cut off by the tone sounding at Leonidas's door.

Lucian lifted an eyebrow. "Expecting someone?"

"No." Leonidas reached out with his fae senses… and tasted lavender and wildberries and crackling magical energy at the door. "Rosalyn." He moved without thinking, heading for the door. Was something wrong? Had she decided to leave already? They hadn't come close to contacting all the vampire covens and making their threat of extinction known, should they infect any more humans with demon essence, much less confronted the fae. It was far too dangerous for her to be out in the world, unguarded—

He used magic to swipe open the front door just before he reached it.

She seemed startled when she saw him.

Which was odd, given *she* was the one showing up unexpectedly.

"Oh, um…" Rosalyn's expression was a weird mixture of embarrassment and confusion. "I can come back later."

What? Rosalyn's gaze flicked past Leonidas's shoulder. He twisted to see Arabella standing behind him.

She was scowling at Rosalyn but reaching for little Larik—Leonidas had almost forgotten he was still holding the baby. "Looks like you have company," Arabella said, lifting the tiny bundle from his arms. "Time for me to put Larik down for a nap anyway." The baby was already asleep, and as far as Leonidas could tell, he never slept in his crib, the one passed down through generations of the House of Smoke—he just got passed from one person to another, 24/7. Everyone wanted to hold the kid. But Arabella was scooting out the door, past Rosalyn's wide-eyed stare, anyway.

Lucian appeared by his side, and his hand landed on Leonidas's shoulder. "Everything okay?" he asked, giving the side-eye to Rosalyn.

The last thing Leonidas needed was his family running her out of the keep by making her uncomfortable. "Yeah, everything's fine. You better go after your mate, though. She's making off with your kid."

Lucian frowned but gave a nod to Rosalyn as he eased out the door and tromped down the hallway.

"Hey," Leonidas said to Rosalyn, frowning a little. "What's up?"

She still seemed flustered. "Okay, that was…" She glanced at Lucian's retreating back, then turned back to Leonidas and bit her lip. "For a second there, I thought you'd somehow made a dragonling overnight."

He huffed a small laugh, although the idea of Larik belonging to him was too close to pain for the laugh to last long. "Dragon pregnancies are crazy fast, but that not fast."

"Yeah?" she asked, curiosity lighting up her eyes. "How fast?"

He frowned. Did she really come visit just to learn dragon trivia? "About six weeks." He swept a look over her —she was back in her normal t-shirt and jeans, the kind that hugged that sexy-fine rear end. Her hair was down. Her eyes were bright. She seemed to have recovered from yesterday's attack. If she was thinking of leaving, it didn't show. "Would you like to come in?" he asked, uncertainly.

She bit her lip again, but the hesitation was brief. "Yeah. I had something I wanted to, um, talk to you about."

He stepped back and gestured her into his lair, but he couldn't help the dread settling on his chest. He contemplated jumping right in and telling her all the reasons she should stay at the keep, but somehow, the words got tangled up as he followed her into the great room.

She gazed around, checking out the artwork on the walls and the pristine couches. Was she judging him about that again? He was utterly lost as to what was happening here.

When she finally faced him, she said, "You really have a beautiful place."

He couldn't help his look of surprise. "You've... seen it before."

The red that flushed her cheeks made him wish he could pull the words back.

"I'm sorry," he said quickly. "I'm just a little, I guess, confused. Please don't tell me you're thinking of leaving the keep because it's just not safe out there, not until we—"

She held up her hand to stop him. "I'm not leaving."

The relief of that was stronger than he expected. His shoulders relaxed. "Okay. Good." He frowned a little. "So what did you want to talk about?"

She got that pinched, hesitating look again. "Did you find a mate, yet?"

"Um... no." That was probably the last thing he expected her to ask. "I've been a little busy." Then it dawned on him she might be concerned about the other women. "But we have made sure all the women who answered the post are safe. Leksander brought the last one in just a little while ago."

She smiled but dropped her gaze. "Of course you did."

He frowned and peered at her, perplexed. "What's this about?"

She looked up at him again, those beautiful blue eyes blazing. "I want to have your baby."

His mouth dropped open. "What?" Then the shock hit his brain and shorted everything out. He literally had no thoughts whatsoever, no words, just a weird numbness that stole over him.

The shock on his face must have been extreme because her face scrunched up, and she stepped back. "Unless you don't want that. *Oh God.* How embarrassing. *Fuck.*" She was cringing and staring at the carpet and… *what did she just say?*

He snapped out of his shock enough to force words out of his mouth. "What are you even talking about?"

"It's just… I thought… *Oh, fuck,* never mind." She made like she would dash past him, heading for the front door.

He caught her as she passed, holding her by the arms and bringing her gently to face him. "Hang on. *Rosalyn.*" He gazed at her, amazed, with a feeling of hope lifting his chest like nothing he'd ever felt. He slid his hands up to her cheeks, magic sparking the entire way. He held her face as he peered into her eyes. "Did you just offer to have my baby?"

She was shaking, a small tremor he could feel in her cheeks. "Would you want that?"

Something shifted inside him. Something hard and real and strong. *Yes, he wanted that.* Very much. He couldn't remember wanting something ever as strongly.

"Yes." It was barely a whisper.

A strange mix of emotions flitted across her face—relief, anxiety, fear. They confused him. Even more so when she reached up and pulled his hands from her cheeks. She held them in hers, but she stepped back and breathed out a shaky breath. Her hands were still quivering.

"Okay." She swallowed. "I can do this for you. The baby thing. Especially, you know, if it's only six weeks. I mean, hell, that's not long, right? And once the baby's born, it's all good, right? Your treaty is settled, you get your five hundred years, all of it. The magic will do it all automatically. Then I can go back to my normal life. Or maybe even, if you have some pull with one of the covens…" She grimaced. "But even if you don't, that's okay. I mean, I want to do this for you, no matter what. Not like some kind of trade. Just… because you've already done so much for me, and…" She faded off at the look on his face.

His heart was sinking with every word. She didn't love him. *She couldn't love him.* He already knew that, but somehow, some stupid part of him had thought… just for a moment…

And yet… she was still willing to do this thing. Carry his child. *For him.*

But of course, she would. Because that was the person Rosalyn Thorne was.

"Sweet Rose," he said, tears threatened the back of his eyes, and the wildness inside him surged up. "It doesn't work that way."

She frowned, scanning his eyes intently. "What doesn't work that way?"

He struggled for words for a moment, just now realizing that he had never explained. Had never had *cause* to explain. Had never thought anything like this would even be in play. *Because the love had to come first.* Or at least it did for any normal person.

But Rosalyn Thorne was extraordinary in every sense of the word.

"You have to *love me*, Rosalyn," he said, his voice thick.

Her expression went from confused to stricken.

The wildness inside him surged. He pushed it back down and pressed on. "The treaty will only work if I can convince someone to fall in love with me… and *then* carry my child. *True Love* is what makes the magic work, you see." Keeping the tears in was causing him actual pain. Like talons slicing through his chest level of pain. "And you don't. I'd feel it—the whole world would feel it—if you did. Because love is magic, at least as far as mating and dragonlings and the treaty is concerned."

"*Oh God,*" she whispered. "Leonidas... I didn't know..."

"I know." He smiled through the pain, but it was getting worse. Like something was inside him, clawing its way out. "You're something else, Rosalyn Thorne. Something... amazing. You're willing to do things that only a fool in love would do—only without the love."

"Well, I *am* a fool," she said, bitterly. "That much is obvious."

"No, you're not." He had to fight to hold himself back. He didn't care if she didn't love him. He didn't care if she never could. He just wanted to take her in his arms and kiss her and somehow, through sheer force of will, generate the magic necessary for her to be his mate anyway. *To carry his baby.* Now that the idea was out there, it was killing him that it wasn't possible. "You're kind. And good. And brave and giving and so fucking sexy. It's a good thing you don't love me because there's no chance in hell I could deserve someone like you."

She seemed horrified by this. "That's not true."

But it was. He knew it deep inside. And even more, he knew he'd do anything to be the man that deserved her. He'd give anything for her, period. Nothing else had ever mattered to him near as much. And that deep-down unshakable truth... shook something loose. It was wild and needy and filled with an insatiable desire...*for her.* Then the last chain holding it down, keeping it locked and leashed... *broke.* He felt it clawing its way out from inside him.

Oh, fuck no.

He staggered back from her. *"Run!"*

Her eyes went wide, but she didn't move.

He roared and turned away from her, spraying dragon-fire across the white couches of his great room as he fought to keep control of the beast... *but it was too late.* The transformation was no normal shift—this was a breaking of bones and ripping of flesh and sundering of mind. He screamed his anger and frustration and all of it, every last shred of his humanity, was worth nothing.

He was wyvern.

And the wildness of his mind, his beast's blind lust and evolutionary need to procreate would send him into a rampage of one thing and one thing only—raping and impregnating any female it could lay its hands on.

No! With his last act of will, he ran straight at the two story windows of his great room and flung himself through. He pumped his wings hard, mustered every spark of magic in his body, and pushed his body to fly at top speed away from the keep. Away from the damage he would cause, the horrors he would propagate, the blood he would spill.

Away from the woman he loved.

He needed to die. Soon.

By everything magic, he would keep her safe... *from him.*

Chapter Sixteen

WHEN THE SCREAM FINALLY DIED—HER SCREAM—ROSALYN ran.

It was a blind burst of terror, out the door of Leonidas's lair, down the hall, running and running away from the *beast* he had become.

Oh God, what did she do?

She couldn't help thinking she'd somehow triggered this—this horrible thing. Something she said or something she did... maybe her magic? She had no idea, but... *Leonidas had turned into a giant, bronze-scaled dragon.* He'd always been a dragon, but now he was... something else. Something wild and horrible. He'd tried to warn her, told her to run, but she'd been frozen in place by fear...

She was running blindly through the hallway, calling for help, hysterical tears streaming down her face until she finally found someone.

Leksander. He was Leonidas's brother, and she remembered him from that first day when he'd tried to make her leave, and she'd fought with him... and Leonidas had rescued her from being thrown out.

Even from the beginning, he was rescuing her.

"Oh God. Oh God." That was all she could get out.

He frowned, taking in the blubbering mess she was. "What's wrong?"

"Leonidas," she gasped. "He's... he's turned into..."

Leksander's face opened in shock. *"Oh no."*

"I was just... he was trying..." God, she couldn't even speak.

"Where is he?" Leksander demanded as he dug in his pocket for something.

"I don't know! He just... *flew..."* Her breath was so ragged, her words were like gasps.

Leksander grabbed hold of her shoulders. *"Where!"*

"In his lair," she managed.

Leksander dropped his hold on her, then raced back down the hallway toward Leonidas's place. He held a phone to his ear and shouted into it. "Leonidas has turned! I'm heading to his lair." Then he swiped off the phone and ran faster.

Rosalyn stood alone, shaking, in the hallway. What could she do? What *should* she do? She was responsible for this, somehow, she just knew it. But she didn't have any magic, she couldn't do anything to help...

She ran down the hallway after Leksander anyway.

When she reached Leonidas's lair, the door was still open, and both his brothers—Lucian and Leksander— were inside. The place was smoldering from the dragonfire Leonidas had let loose, black scorches marring half the pure-white couches and carpet and décor. The giant, jagged hole left in the windows let in a rush of cool mountain air that chilled Rosalyn to the bone.

She stood there at the entrance to the great room as Leksander cursed in a language she didn't understand and paced in front of the window. Lucian was a little more calm—he noticed her first. He lurched over to her side so fast, she stumbled backward, afraid he might take out his anger on her.

But he only gripped her arm to keep her from falling. "What happened?"

"I… I'm sorry," she said.

"You fucking should be!" Leksander screeched from across the room.

She shuddered with the vehemence in his voice.

"Shut the fuck up, Leksander!" More quietly, but no less intently, he said to her. "I shouldn't have asked what happened. That was a stupid question. I *know* what happened. What I need to know is *when.*"

"When?" she asked, dazed.

"How long since he turned?" he clarified, speaking slowly like she was dim or slow or couldn't understand what he was saying.

It roused a touch of anger that fought through the shock. "Just a minute. Maybe two."

He twisted to shout at Leksander. "Go after him! He can't be far."

Leksander roared and then shifted into a huge silver dragon and leaped through the broken window, shattering it more and raining shards down into the forest below.

Rosalyn just stared after him. *They really were dragons.* She knew it, but this was the first time she was seeing it with her own eyes.

Lucian forced her attention back. "You need to stay at the keep, Rosalyn," he said tightly. "He'll come after you, wherever you go. You're safer here."

"*Why?*" She was crumpling inside. What had she done? And why would Lucian imply Leonidas would hurt her? She couldn't imagine it… but then that thing he turned into was fucking crazy.

Lucian gave her a pitying look. "He didn't tell you. Of course not."

"Tell me *what?*" she demanded. Tears were springing out of their own accord—she couldn't tell if they were from fear or panic or guilt.

"He's *cursed*, Rosalyn," he said, his voice surprisingly soft. "By a witch. Cursed to never love another woman. And if he did…"

Her eyes went wide. "This is because of me?" Her voice squeaked, but she knew it even before she said it. She *knew* she was responsible. But her mouth was hanging open because she was just now figuring out why.

Leonidas loved her.

Lucian's pinched look was all he had for a response to that. He stepped back and pulled out his phone, tapping a fast number in. "I'll get Cinaed to guard you while I go after him," he said quickly then turned away to speak into the phone.

She stared mutely at the giant hole in Leonidas's window. He'd been cursed by a witch, and now he'd fallen in love with one. All her tricks. All her lies. Even her offer to try to fix it… somehow, it had triggered his curse and turned him into a horrible beast.

A beast Lucian said would come hunting for her.

She'd done nothing but lie to Leonidas all the way along…

And now his beast might kill her for it.

Leonidas's story is just beginning…

SEDUCED BY A DRAGON

(Fallen Immortals 5)

Grab Seduced by a Dragon today!

Subscribe to Alisa's newsletter

for new releases and giveaways

http://smarturl.it/AWsubscribeBARDS

Paranormal Romance Series by Alisa Woods

https://alisawoodsauthor.com/

DOT COM WOLVES

The Big Bad Wolf… is her boss.

RIVERWISE PRIVATE SECURITY

Three hot brothers fighting to keep wolf shifters safe.

WILDING PACK WOLVES

The ex-Army bodyguard of a beautiful heiress has a secret.

FALLEN IMMORTALS

A hot Dragon Prince needs a mate, before he turns feral.

FALLEN ANGELS

He's Guardian of a beautiful scientist and oh so Tempted.

LEGAL MAGICK

An incubus FBI agent, a billionaire witch, and someone spiking street drugs with deadly magic.

BROKEN SOULS

She's stumbled into the lair of desperate dragon shifters… and she's just what the Lord of the Lair needs.

To be the first to hear about new releases…

Subscribe to Alisa's Newsletter

https://alisawoodsauthor.com/free-story/

About the Author

Alisa Woods lives in the Midwest with her husband and family, but her heart will always belong to the beaches and mountains where she grew up. She writes sexy paranormal romances about complicated men and the strong women who love them. Her books explore the struggles we all have, where we resist—and succumb to—our most tempting vices as well as our greatest desires. No matter the challenge, Alisa firmly believes that hearts can mend and love will triumph over all.

www.AlisaWoodsAuthor.com